THE
LONG
RIDE

THE
LONG
RIDE

MARINA BUDHOS

WENDY
LAMB
BOOKS

Text copyright © 2019 by Marina Budhos
Jacket art copyright © 2019 by Rebecca Glendining

Visit us on the Web! rhcbooks.com

Educators and librarians, for a variety of teaching tools, visit us at RHTeachersLibrarians.com

Library of Congress Cataloging-in-Publication Data
Names: Budhos, Marina Tamar, author.
Title: The long ride / Marina Budhos.
Description: First edition. | New York : Wendy Lamb Books, an imprint of Random House Children's Books, [2019] | Summary: In New York in 1971, Jamila and Josie are bused across Queens where they try to fit in at a new, integrated junior high school while their best friend, Francesca, tests the limits at a private school. | Identifiers: LCCN 2018041547 (print) | LCCN 2018047945 (ebook) | ISBN 978-0-553-53424-5 (ebook) | ISBN 978-0-553-53422-1 (trade) | ISBN 978-0-553-53423-8 (lib. bdg.)
Subjects: | CYAC: School integration—Fiction. | Friendship—Fiction. | Junior high schools—Fiction. | Schools—Fiction. | Race relations—Fiction. | Racially mixed people—Fiction. | Queens (New York, N.Y.)—History—20th century—Fiction.
Classification: LCC PZ7.B8827 (ebook) | LCC PZ7.B8827 Lon 2019 (print) | DDC [Fic]—dc23

The text of this book is set in 12.5-point Adobe Garamond.
Interior design by Betty Lew

Printed in the United States of America
10 9 8 7 6 5 4 3 2 1
First Edition

IN MEMORY OF MY MOTHER,
SHIRLEY ZALTZMAN BUDHOS

QUEENS,
NEW YORK CITY,
1971

PROLOGUE

BOOTS

It's a hot June afternoon, three days before sixth grade graduation. My two best friends, Francesca and Josie, are sitting with me in Francesca's bedroom, chatting about the new junior high all the way across Queens.

Francesca's room is the nicest—she has a spiraling rattan headboard, a shag rug and matching beanbag chair. We're already munching on our favorite snack: Cheez Doodles dipped in cream cheese.

"Why do we have to go so far?" Josie asks, sipping a ginger ale.

"Integration," I say. I test the word in my mouth.

"What's that mean?" Josie asks.

"Everyone will look more like us," Francesca says.

We've always been different from the other kids in our neighborhood: our skin nut brown and coppery and dark brown. In the class pictures we're the smudges that somehow stand out or make a grandmother's smile go stiff. *Oh, that's nice. Where's she from?*

Francesca is unusual-pretty: gray-green eyes like her mother's, set in a tawny face; frizzy gold-brown hair with a hint of kink. She shifts around in her looks like a tabby cat. And then there's her full mouth, and a body that seems much older than mine. Sometimes when we page through our magazines and giggle, I think, *I can see Francesca there, one day.*

"It's going to be so great!" Francesca says now. "We're going to be so popular!"

Josie makes a face. "I don't care about that."

Josie's the quiet one of us. She does her hair in two tight braids, wears old-fashioned dresses, her thin gold cross dangling over Peter Pan collars.

"Watch." I jump from the bed and strut, draping a towel over my hair and pretending to toss it over my shoulders. "Oh, hi. Sorry, I can't hang out. I'm so-oo busy."

Francesca and Josie fall over laughing.

"I know what we have to do!" Francesca says. "We have to wear the same boots."

"Oh yeah, like the song!"

When we were little, I used to play Nancy Sinatra's "These Boots Are Made for Walkin' " and I'd prance around in my own shiny go-go boots.

"Only let's get this kind." Francesca pulls out an issue

4

of *Tiger Beat*. In the picture two girls are standing back to back, arms crossed, bandanas tied around their necks, and wearing orange construction boots.

"We'll wear them the first day!"

"Promise?" Francesca asks.

We make our vow: Me and Josie and Francesca will wear the same orange construction boots. We'll stand at the bus stop and put together our toes so they make a three-petal flower. Then we'll march into our new school, where there will be more kids who look like us.

*　*　*

We convince our parents that we want to buy matching boots for our twelfth birthdays—Francesca and me are in August, and Josie is in September. We have to do it before Francesca leaves for England to see her grandparents, as she does every year. At Thompson's shoe store we find the exact style: orange tie-up construction boots, a seam of white stitching like tiny rice around the rim. We each slip them on.

"Make sure they have enough room," Josie's mother says. "You girls are growing." She took us down here since we're not allowed to go on public buses by ourselves yet.

I like the feel of these boots: the stiff leather, strong and sturdy. I'm sure I can march anywhere.

We bump hips. "Here we come!" Francesca shouts in the middle of the store.

"Hush," Josie says, but I can see she's pleased.

When we step outside with our packages, the muggy air hits us. The Jamaica Avenue el train shrieks overhead, making slashing shadows of dark and light. We're so happy with our new boots, we skip the whole way to the bus stop. We are ready.

PART 1

CHAPTER 1

WE THE DREAM

Twelve is the best and twelve is the worst.

It's the breathless swoop at the top of the Ferris wheel, dangling and wishing you could stay. It's the moment when the wheel's about to drop, and you're scared, but it's thrilling too.

Because twelve is when you clutch for everything to stay the same. But it's also when you're tipped forward, ready for something new.

In the spring of sixth grade, our last year in elementary school, Francesca and Josie and me like to lean against the schoolyard fence and stare at the kids in front of the junior high across the street. Girls with long straight hair that swings at their butts. That's going to be us! But how will I ever get from here to there? I still play with Josie's dollhouse. I'm afraid of the dark. I sort of giggle about

9

boys, but really I wish they'd leave us alone. When I think about thirteen and having a chest that shows beneath my shirt, my stomach hurts. I wish I could stay right here, fingers on the diamonds of twisted metal, looking out.

Almost-twelve is when I learn about our new school. When everything changes in Queens, and in New York City.

One day I come home with a mimeographed flyer.

"What's this?" My mother starts reading. Her light brown hair is drawn back into a ponytail. Daddy always says that Mom still looks like the twenty-year-old he met studying at a coffee shop near Columbia University.

"It's called a pairing."

"What's that mean?"

"The seventh graders will go to another school, a new one, in South Jamaica."

"Why on earth? Our junior high is just a few blocks away!"

"Integration."

Mom looks at Daddy standing in the door. He nods. *Integration.*

Integration. That's a good thing. One of those banner words that snaps brightly over our heads. Last year we did a dance about Martin Luther King Jr. in the gymnasium, all the girls in maroon Danskins. We listened to the "I Have a Dream" speech crackling on speakers. *My four little children will one day live in a nation where they will not be judged by the color of their skin . . .*

Integration is what our family does in quiet and private ways. Mom grew up on Long Island, the daughter of a policeman; she met Daddy when she was studying social work, and he was an engineering student living in Harlem. When her brother, Joe, heard she was dating a man from Barbados, he showed up at her apartment, tapping a crowbar against his palm. Daddy gently invited him to eat *keema* that he'd cooked for Mom. Uncle Joe laughs now, says that he had to like a guy who cooked for his sister. Still, no one in the family came when they got married at city hall.

Two nights after getting the flyer, Daddy and Mom go to the school meeting, Mom with her cardigan draped over her shoulders and a pleated skirt. Daddy in his usual suit and tie. My parents always get dressed up. One of Mom's many rules for me and my brother, Karim: "You have to give a certain kind of impression because they're not used to families like us." Meaning a tall black man with a hint of East Indian in his face, and his pale, thin wife.

I'm finishing my homework when they come back, arguing softly in the living room about the new plan.

"It's not that bad," my mother says.

"Penny, I didn't work so hard and get myself out of a village school for my daughter to go to school in a poor neighborhood. That's going backward."

"It's all new teachers," Mom says. "A new building."

"But why now?"

11

"Our schools are as segregated as ever."

He sighs. "I know. But have you ever driven by those streets? The boarded-up windows?" He shakes his head. "My child is not an experiment."

"If those words came out of our neighbors, you'd be upset."

"There's a difference."

"Is there?"

He doesn't answer.

*　*　*

Me and Josie and Francesca, our families, we're a link of firsts. No one ever says that exactly. Francesca's mom, Mrs. George, who has strawberry-blond hair and high cheekbones, and was once a model, often boasts how her husband was the first "someone of his background, growing up on the wrong side of Philadelphia, to sell fine antiques." He even opened his own shop on the Upper East Side in Manhattan with "the very best quality." And Daddy was the first one in his family to move off his island to become a geologist and an engineer.

Josie's dad, Mr. Rivera, who wears the same cotton shirts with the big embroidered pockets that my dad likes, has the best "first" story. Mr. Rivera is light-skinned—"café con leche, with lots of the leche," he teases—while Mrs. Rivera, who grew up on the island of Jamaica, is ebony dark. When the Riveras first came to the rental office here in Cedar Gardens, they were told there were no apartments, and to check back. Every other Monday at nine a.m. Mr. Rivera would call. After a whole year of calling he just showed up at the office. That very day, an old couple who was retiring to Florida had come to hand in their keys. "Why, thank you," Mr. Rivera said, holding his palm open. The Riveras were the first nonwhite family to live in Cedar Gardens.

We moved in a few years later. Francesca's family came next and bought the Tudor across the street from our garden apartments. Mr. George said he always dreamed of owning a house like that, and Mrs. George said it reminded her of England. Francesca told me that six months after they moved in, two For Sale signs went up on the block. The first time my mother and father showed up for a block party with a casserole, Daddy said, "You shoulda seen their mouths drop open!" He wasn't laughing the time we had the N-word scrawled on our milk box, the bottles broken. Or the time a group of boys chased my brother, Karim, home with stones. He still has a tiny pale scar over his right eye.

Our mothers met in the playground, pushing us on swings, watching our older brothers. "If I have a son," Mrs. George said to Mrs. Rivera, "I hope he looks like yours."

Our parents always tell us: Don't wander too far. Stay close, where we can find you. They never say why exactly.

13

But we know. The hot stares from stoops. The neighbor who called the police on Mr. George when they saw him unlocking his own door. Josie's brother, Manuel, getting chased home from school with boys calling, "Run fast, chocolate bunny!" The worst was when another family like us moved in and someone slipped a lit rag in their basement window. Our dads went over to talk; my mom and Mrs. Rivera made casseroles for the neighbors. But that family didn't stay long.

Once, I was with my mother buying groceries, when the cashier said, "She's your daughter? I thought maybe she was your maid's girl!"

"Are you blind?" I blurted. "We have the same face!"

I know I shouldn't shoot my mouth off. But it stung. After, my mother told me, "Jamila, don't ever let something like that get to you. She's a girl who will never go to college."

That's my parents' answer for everything: grades and school. That will shield you from the hurts from people who aren't ready for us.

*   *   *

All through the spring, mimeographs about the school plan whisper through the mail slot. One night Mrs. Rowan knocks on the door to ask Mom to sign a protest letter against the school plan. She says that a lot of parents are talking about leaving the city. My mom's green eyes go hard under the porch light and she jams her arms across

14

her chest. My mother looks delicate, but there's something firm in her, like marble. My parents would never move—my mother says that over her dead body would she ever move back to the suburbs. The next day, Daddy goes to see the new school and he's really impressed with the labs. "You'll dissect real fetal pigs!"

"That's gross!" I cry, but I'm glad to see Daddy pleased.

That evening, the dads get together at our place. They sit out on the concrete patio, their voices lifting and twining around each other: Mr. Rivera's rapid-fire words, my father's lilt, Mr. George's deep boom. There's an ease among them, even though Mr. George leads a fancier life, going to England or France to buy antiques.

"Who's my daughter going to date?" Mr. Rivera asks. He's wolfing down Mrs. Rivera's fruitcake, which everyone agrees is the best they have ever tasted. "Boys who will never go to college?"

"But who is your daughter going to date here?" Daddy points out.

"She won't date." He grins. "That's what I like."

*   *   *

At sixth grade graduation, Mom lets me wear matching hot pants and top. But I still have to put on long white knee socks. The auditorium is so warm the seats stick to the backs of our thighs. After we sing "This Land Is Your Land" and "Aquarius/Let the Sunshine In," Mr. Beale, our principal, gets up and tells us what a great accomplishment graduating from sixth grade is; and even though there's a lot of uncertainty about next year, he's excited for us to be part of "a grand new experiment."

"You are our future!" he declares.

Then we stream outside to sign our yearbooks. Three girls in my class are moving away to Westchester and Long Island because of the busing plan. Other families are sending their kids to Catholic school. One, Susan Green, wrote on my name, *I'll always remember you! Please come visit me!* The parents stand talking along the edges of the yard, faces folded in worry.

Me and Josie and Francesca swap secret smiles. This school is for us. Where we can belong. We have our boots sitting in boxes in our closets. We'll put them on, link arms, and be the dream.

*   *   *

A few weeks later Francesca calls a meeting. This time we're in Josie's bedroom, sitting on the floor next to the dollhouse her father built. Francesca looks quiet, her hands folded in her lap. Usually she and I are sped up and snatching words from each other. Josie is the calm one, taking her time.

"So, guys, I hate to tell you. My parents—" She pauses. "They put a deposit on private school."

"What?" Josie looks stunned.

"Where?"

"In Manhattan. My dad knew someone who got me

in." She adds, "They say they can't take a chance. It's hard enough for me as it is."

"It's not fair!" I say. Tears prick my eyes. "You should be with us." I can't imagine junior high without Francesca. We're like three different pieces that fit together, perfectly. Even when we fight.

"I know! It's not even my idea. I want to be with you guys. But my parents didn't want me to go to—" Her nose wrinkles.

I bite my lip. And it's okay for *us*?

We cry. We complain about all the things we won't be able to do together: Meet new kids from a different neighborhood. Chat with cute boys. March together down the halls in magic coolness. Talk back to bossy Lucy Nelson. Whisper about Joey Marshall, who is okay, but he can be so dopey. Carry spiral notebooks and write only in pen. We promise that even though we're not all in the same place, we'll always check in with each other and never stop being together.

The night before our first day, Josie and I decide that we'll still wear our construction boots. Even though we're only two.

We'll still be the dream.

CHAPTER 2

BUS

First day of seventh grade.

In our construction boots.

Taking a bus.

And for the first time ever, Francesca isn't with us.

My stomach's tap-tapping like a drum. A lot of families are at the bus stop, which is weird. Junior high is when you're supposed to walk off, no more parents watching you like kindergarten babies. But there are the Siegels, patting Jill on her tiny shoulders. Joey Marshall is marching up with both his parents, a new army satchel slanted across his chest. I just have my dad here, standing thin and tall behind us. Josie's mom is there too, in one of her housedresses. She's the only one smiling.

"It's late," Josie says.

"Not really." But my stomach's jumping.

"How long is the ride?" Mrs. Rowan asks.

"About forty minutes," my father offers. "I used to take Jamila there for tennis lessons. Do you know Springfield Gardens?"

"No." Mrs. Rowan is curt.

I stare at the ground. The backs of my ears seem to sweat. I know what she means: We don't go there, to the black side. My family and Josie's and Francesca's have to live with these knife-words said, and not said, all the time.

My father looks down at his suede shoes. He's dressed for work: tweed blazer, skinny navy tie. Two mechanical pencils are clipped to his blazer pocket. "The new school is in good shape," he says.

"Yeah, but try walking across the street without getting mugged by them!" Mr. Rowan laughs.

Them.

Josie and I freeze and move closer together. This is why Josie and Francesca and I can be best friends. We don't have to explain to each other who we are.

"Ah, come on. Kids are kids everywhere. Even if they're green or purple. Pains in the butt." Mr. Marshall ruffles Joey's hair. He's a jolly father, who never gets mad.

"Hey, kiddo." I feel a playful swat on my head.

"Hey!" I turn.

It's my brother, Karim, on his way to high school. He's with Josie's brother, Manuel, who's puffed his hair out into an Afro, and two girls, who I'm happy to see are wearing the same style boots as us, only these girls don't look sweaty.

Daddy frowns at Karim's jean jacket and frayed bell-bottoms. "That's what you're wearing today?"

Karim winks at me. "Go for it, kiddo. Make your mark at your new school."

I grin. I like and don't like his nickname for me, which makes me feel like I'm a tagalong. But I do want to be like Karim and his friends. Brave. Fist the air. Shout slogans.

"Go on," my father says to Karim.

"It's here!" Mrs. Siegel cries.

A big yellow school bus is turning the corner, grinding toward us, with its bug-eyed headlights. A few kids in the back stare wanly through the windows. My father bends down and whispers, "Make sure you're in the SP program, yes?"

"Yes, Daddy." SP is the special program for the junior high advanced track. Usually you'd know if you made it in by now, but the new school said we'd get our assignments on the first day.

As we start to inch toward the bus, Josie pokes me. "Look, it's Francesca!"

We turn as Francesca flies down her stoop and comes running toward us. She's in a uniform: blue pleated skirt, gray knee socks, white blouse, and a blue cardigan. Her frizzy hair is clipped with a barrette on both sides, making two funny poofs over her ears. Not our Francesca, who loves her embroidered peasant blouses and bell-bottoms. And she's got an expensive bag—like a leather briefcase with straps.

"Francesca!" Mr. George, tall and movie-star handsome next to his convertible, is jingling his keys. "Come on, darlin'," he calls. "We're late!"

"Sorry!" Francesca grabs our arms. "Let's talk after school, okay? Compare notes?"

"Yeah," Josie and I mumble.

Francesca gives our arms another squeeze. "Tell me who's cute?"

Then she runs across the street and ducks into the car, nodding to her father, who holds open the door like she's a model. And that's when I notice Francesca's shoes: they're shiny black with just a hint of a heel. The car slides away, to Manhattan, to a world I can't see.

Josie and I are left behind.

CHAPTER 3

BRAND-NEW

When the bus heaves off, it's like I'm in a boat that's jolted from the pier. My father's face looks so small, his horn-rimmed glasses glinting in the sunlight. His mouth is tight, not really smiling. And then we swerve around the corner and rumble away from the side street into traffic.

I perch on the edge of the lumpy seat, press my forehead against the window. Josie's beside me, her two neat braids tucked behind her ears. We leave our part of Queens, which has houses with front lawns or garden apartments around grassy courtyards, then cross the borough to where everything becomes more pressed together: Small houses on tight lots. Apartment buildings. And the faces change, turning darker, more like mine. Sometimes Daddy and I come down here to visit his old friends, or pick up meat patties, which he misses from his home in Barbados.

Josie points to a big stone building with a sign out front. "That's our church."

Sundays are the only time I see Mrs. Rivera dressed up. She and Josie usually have matching outfits that Mrs. Rivera sews. Josie says, "It's the loud and singing kind."

Now I ask, "Do you like it there?"

"Some. I like the cookies and punch after and the study group."

"Anyone cute?"

She shrugs. "The boys there are very clean."

"What does that mean?"

"They don't curse."

I always feel as if Josie has another life on the other side of Jamaica Avenue that she disappears into.

Finally the bus comes to a stop. The first thing I notice when we filter down the steps is a hoe and a tractor sitting in a field at the side of the school, next to a huge mound of dirt. The building is made of beige brick and steel, with checkerboard windows, decals still on the panes. Kids swarm all over, shouting, pouring in the front doors. A few cluster around us, staring, as we try to make our way to the front steps.

"You from that other school?" someone asks.

"Yeah," Joey says.

"How far away?"

"Far."

"How long the bus take?" A girl plants herself in front of Joey.

"Long," he mumbles.

"How long?"

He shrugs and then her friend asks, "Where you get that bag from? It's nice."

"The Army Navy store."

A tall woman with a walkie-talkie shoulders her way in. She's wearing a crimson dress, and a crown of braids tops her head. Her voice rolls out, rich and commanding. "Now, is that the way to greet our new friends?"

Some kids look at their feet. "No."

"No what?"

"No, Mrs. Johnson."

"That's more like it."

They scatter up the stairs as she turns to us. What a sorry troop we must be, in our wilted new clothes, with our shy eyes. She booms, "Welcome, welcome to JHS 241, boys and girls! Don't just stand there! Go on, get to the auditorium and join the other seventh graders!"

We stare at her until Jill offers, "But we don't know where that is."

"So you don't." She laughs. "You won't know where a lot of things are. Just head on in and turn to the right. Follow the signs. You'll figure it out."

Inside, sound bounces off the shiny wall tiles, swelling around me as we join a river of kids surging through the auditorium doors and down the aisles. Me and Josie try to stay close, but we're shoved from all sides. A boy's heel stamps my toe. "Hey!" I yell. My construction boot is ruined by a heel-shaped smudge. I want to cry right there.

We hurry into the first seats we can find. Joey and the rest scoot in too. The seats are so smooth, we nearly slip off. The boys slide low down until their knees bang the backs of the seats in front of them. Shouts swirl around us. "Hey, girl." "Hey! How you been?" "Good. Your summer?" "My momma took us down to my grandmother's. You? You see Gerald? You see his sister?" "Yeah." The kids from our neighborhood make up about four rows, and everyone else is from around here, all in skin tones like mine and Josie's.

Then it hits me: I can finally blend, but I don't know anyone from here. These kids have known each other their whole lives.

A hush falls on the group in front of us as a tall girl saunters down the aisle. Tight-cropped hair. Gold hoop earrings bounce at her neck. She can't be in seventh grade. She slides into her seat, places her bag on her lap. It isn't a satchel, but a pocketbook. *Johanna, Johanna,* the girls sing out. She serves them a frosty smile.

One boy tilts forward across the aisle. "When you coming my way?"

"Never."

She swivels her head, showing her cool eyes. The boy stares at his hands.

25

Lucy Nelson leans in and says to the whole row, "My mom says this place isn't going to last. That by Christmas we'll be back at the school we're *supposed* to go to."

"Some parents aren't going to send their kids at all," someone else says.

"Well, that's stupid," I say.

Lucy peers at me. I scrunch down in my seat. Sometimes I have a big mouth, but other times I just want to hide. I can't tell which part of me is ready to come out.

I feel like my old life is sliding away. Cedar Gardens, the playground where my palms sting from punchball, or the little slant of shade where me and Francesca and Josie used to gather to watch the boys play basketball. What's ahead: turning thirteen, fourteen, girls with curves who carry pocketbooks. I put my hand right next to Josie's, set it on the armrest, to steady myself.

That's all that matters: Josie.

* * *

A bald man strides onto the stage and starts tapping a microphone. Then comes Mrs. Johnson, who warns, "Boys and girls, we can do this the easy way or . . . the *hard* way." The word—*hard*—is low and throbbing mad. Boys stop kicking. Girls settle into quiet.

"Thank you," she says dryly.

The bald man is our principal: Mr. Stotter. He has pink, shiny cheeks and is shorter than Mrs. Johnson. Sweat patches show through his suit jacket.

He smiles. "Thank you, Mrs. Johnson. Today is not just the beginning of junior high. It's the beginning of a great dream that you all get to be a part of."

Everyone looks at each other, twists in their seats. It's embarrassing when adults talk like this.

"Now let's all give a warm welcome to our new friends, who have come all the way from north Queens!" He gestures to our rows.

Noise spurts up: clapping and screaming, whistling, banging the new seats. But no one is really welcoming us. I don't blame them.

More speeches roll out. The head of phys ed says they are doing an experiment and the girls get to do "modern dance," in addition to gym, while the boys get an extra period of basketball. And there will be real elections for school officers. Josie nudges me. "Maybe you should do that," she whispers.

Mr. Stotter introduces a Miss Griffith from the guidance department. At first I think she's a student. She's got a teased-out Afro, a shirred blouse tucked into low-hipped pants, and cork-bottom sandals. She gives a wave, bracelets tinkling on her wrists. "Hey, guys."

Seats bang, hands wave, and chatter bubbles up again.

"Hey!" a boy calls out from the back. "When we get out of here?"

"When do we get lunch?" another kid yells.

Mrs. Johnson glares. "Your name, young man?"

"Darren. Darren Paul."

27

"Okay, Darren Paul. I don't know you. But I do hope I'll be getting to know your good side in the next three years. Understand?"

He nods. "Yes."

"Yes what?" She taps her name tag.

"Yes, Mrs. Johnson." Miss Griffith steps forward. "That's okay. No need for punishment." She comes to the edge of the stage and leans over, smiling. "You guys are really lucky. You're part of something brand-new. A completely different kind of school, where children from all walks of life are brought together. So we're going to play a game. Teachers are going to come to the end of your row and direct some of you to move to another place. That way you'll sit with unfamiliar students. And you're going to introduce yourselves."

Groans erupt as half the auditorium stands and shuffles into new seats. It's like watching a quilt being threaded a different way. Luckily, me and Josie manage to stay together.

"Now, everyone. Introduce yourself to the person next to you and say one thing about yourself."

When Josie starts chatting away to a pretty girl on her left, I turn to a boy on my right. "I'm Jamila."

"Uh-huh."

"What's your name?"

"Darren." It's that boy who spoke up.

I ask, "What's one thing you can tell me about yourself?"

He lifts his face. He's narrow-boned, with bright, mischievous eyes and a pointy chin. "I like your friend."

I blink. Josie? Francesca's the one the boys notice, especially this summer in her cutoffs.

"Now you're supposed to ask about me," I say.

He grins. "You're feisty."

"Good word," I say with a smile.

"Thanks, Teach."

Miss Griffith calls, "Now everyone shake your neighbor's hand!"

Darren shakes mine once, then pushes his hand under his armpit.

"There." Miss Griffith laughs. "That wasn't so bad, was it?"

Darren and I are sort of laughing ourselves. Maybe I can make new friends here. Someone on the other side of him is jiggling back and forth on his seat. Josie whispers, "I think he wants to meet you too."

"Who?"

"That other boy."

He's craning his neck to get around Darren and now I can see him better. He's got melting brown eyes and the sweetest, longest smile. Heat brushes my insides. He's still smiling when he turns away.

The bell lets out a long bleat. "Wait, wait, boys and girls!" Mr. Stotter shouts into the microphone. "We are going to call your row and you will walk—I said *walk*—to the very back, where there are five tables. One of those tables has the first letter of your last name and your homeroom teacher's name. First two rows, go!"

It's bedlam. Me and Josie are mashed up against a moving wall of arms and legs. I'm "C" for Clarke and she's "R" for Rivera so we can't stay together. Finally I'm at a table and the lady hands me a slip of paper.

Jamila Clarke
Miss Fine. SP Homeroom: 219,
Science Lab.

Clutching my slip, I try to find Josie. The speakers blare: "You have two minutes to get to your homeroom! Two minutes!"

I search the bobbing heads for her braids. "Josie?" I call. There's a swirl of strange kids, and Josie is gone.

CHAPTER 4

OBJECTIVE-SUBJECTIVE

"I can show you where to go."

I look up as someone in the stairwell shoves past me. It's him. The boy with melting eyes.

"I'm John." He looks shyly at his feet.

"I'm Jamila."

"You want me to show you your homeroom?"

"How do you know where to go?" I ask.

"They gave us a tour last week." He adds, "I live near here."

I follow him up the stairs and down a hall. John is wearing a checked shirt that's pressed at the sleeves, tucked into his trousers. A lot of girls call out to him as he weaves his way. "Hey, John!" But they say it *Jo-ohn,* their voices curling and stretching. Like they know something about him, some kind of deep secret.

31

When we get to Room 219, he looks very pleased.

"Thanks," I say. Then I blush. "Are you in the same class?"

He tips his head. "Just across."

Behind him, Darren is sauntering down the hall. "Hey, John, man, what you doing there? That's not your room!"

"See you," John says quietly. But he doesn't move.

I want to stay too, but Miss Fine, my homeroom teacher, is waving to me. "Bye," I whisper, and duck into my room.

Homeroom is just like Daddy said the school would be: so new, I can smell fresh paint. We're in a lab, so we sit on stools, and the tops of our tables are thick black slabs. I look around and see the kids I've always gone to school with. Only a few new faces—including that tall girl Johanna and José, who wears a grown-up tan blazer and a bow tie. Josie's not here. She's in a different SP homeroom.

Miss Fine has an open face and eyes that seem to snap open, with spiky lashes like a doll's. A lot of the teachers are young. "I'll have all of you for biology," Miss Fine explains. "So I'm going to get to know you really, really well."

She passes out a map of the school and a little notebook with a blue line running down the middle. "Seventh grade is really different from elementary school. You don't have one teacher. You have many. The bell rings and you go off to different classes, to learn individual subjects.

That can feel like a lot of compartments. Nothing connects." She gives us an eager smile.

"Since this is a brand-new school, we can try out new ideas and ways of learning. I want your homeroom to not just be the place where we take attendance. I want this to be the place where you can put it all together. To *synthesize*."

Then she writes on the blackboard:

Objective
Subjective

"I am a science teacher. In science, facts are objective. But I value both parts of knowing: objective and subjective." She points to our notebooks. "In those notebooks, I'd like you to look around and record *what* you see. That will go in the left side. On the other side, I'd like you to record what you *feel* about what you see. Whatever you want to share, you can, during homeroom. But only what you want. The rest is private."

Everyone is busy. A few of the boys look at their notebooks, faces scrunched, as if wishing this work would go away. I have no idea what to write. Usually when I write in my diary, I draw too.

So on the left side I draw a picture of her, and I write: *Miss Fine is pretty. She wears mascara. Her ankles are thick so that makes her look plainer.*

That feels mean. And it isn't very objective. So I add:

Everything is new here. Even the stairs smell of new paint. The walls are really clean.

On the right side, the one labeled *Subjective*, I stare. I write: *How am I going to fit into all this?*

*   *   *

The rest of the morning is more of the same—the same kids, shooting through the halls as if in a space capsule. I scan for Josie but never see her. By lunchtime my new boots are scuffed up, my hair in humid, itchy waves. When I finally see Josie my whole body relaxes. Just having her beside me as we push our trays along the runners feels good. "We aren't in any of the same classes!"

"I know."

"Who do you have for homeroom?" I ask.

"I forget her name."

"Joey's in mine. He is so annoying!"

She nods to the lunch counter. "What are you getting?"

We both stare at the offerings: what looks like baloney sandwiches or too-yellow mac and cheese. I take a sandwich and she does too, along with a cup of Jell-O and a carton of milk.

"Want to compare schedules?" I ask as we sit. "Maybe we have some electives together."

She shrugs, but we spread our schedules on the table. Every day is different until we get to Thursday. "Look!" I say. "We have Community Circle."

She gives a small smile. "What's that even mean?"

We barely have time to scarf down our sandwiches before we're herded out to the yard.

Girls clump in big groups, some boys are over by the handball courts and others shoot hoops. None of these seem like places for us. So we find a corner bench. Before I can ask her, "Where's your homeroom and who are your teachers and who's in your classes?" two boys stroll up. It's John, with Darren behind. I feel Josie sit up a little beside me.

"You find the rest of your rooms okay?" John asks.

"Not really. It's easy to get lost."

"So Teach doesn't know everything," Darren says.

"Very funny." I'm turning warm all over, under my shirt collar and spreading across my face. I've never felt anything like it. Does Josie notice?

"You ask him his last name?" Darren asks. "It's Wayne. John Wayne. You know who that is?"

"Of course I do!"

"He look like a cowboy to you?"

"No."

"Me neither. What's your name?" he asks Josie, but she just stares at the ground.

"You don't wanna talk to me?"

"No."

I look at her, surprised. Josie's always so kind to everyone. Now she's sitting very straight, chin tipped up, staring right through Darren to the handball courts. As if she doesn't want anyone or anything to touch her.

"Aw, come on!"

"It's Josie." Then she adds, "That's for Josefina."

Now I'm stunned. Josie never uses that name. Only her mother does, when she's mad and calls out, "Josefina, you get in this house right now!" Or her father trills in Spanish, "¡Josefina, vamos!"

"Josefina," Darren repeats.

The bell sounds out. John throws me a slow smile, and I'm bathed in quiet warmth.

*   *   *

"Well, that was the worst day ever," Lucy Nelson declares as we stream out the front doors and head toward the bus. "I can't believe I have to be in this school for three years."

Josie and I exchange looks. "It's not so bad," I say.

"Oh really? Tell me one kid that was nice to you today. Except for when they had to do that dumb exercise. How embarrassing!" Lucy is blunt and always declaring things. When she didn't invite me to her fifth grade skating party, I decided we're officially not friends.

"I talked to two boys," I say. "They were funny and nice. And they showed me to my room."

Josie smiles. "John did."

"Who's he?" Lucy asks.

"A really nice boy," I reply.

As the doors fold shut, Danny Rowan calls out, "Lock your windows!"

Joey doffs him in the back of the head. "Stupid!"

I start to jump up, ready to take on Danny and Lucy. Shove them, hard. Josie yanks me back down. "Forget it," she whispers.

The bus starts to rumble away. We cross Jamaica Avenue, back toward our lawns and big, full trees. I'm still mad. It's like something has sliced me in two. Only when my shoulder bumps into Josie do I feel whole.

CHAPTER 5

SP FOR SPECIAL

The minute I get home I race upstairs and strip off my clothes, which stick to me like another skin. I kick off my heavy boots. A blister has puffed at the back of each ankle.

In the mirror, I check to see if I'm different, officially in seventh grade. I'm still too skinny with no hips and ash-smudge knees. My eyebrows look like thick caterpillars over a beaked nose. But I've got black wavy hair from my grandma Rashida, Dad's Indian side. My hair is growing out, and is starting to drape past my shoulders.

Once Josie comes over, we open cold Tabs, suck them down, and hurry across the street to find out about Francesca's first day.

She throws open the door. "Oh my god, guys, I have

so much to tell you!" She squeezes both our wrists and then we run upstairs and sit cross-legged on her bed.

"So what's it like?" I ask.

"It's so beautiful. They have lounges! With beanbag chairs! Can you imagine? We have a period just to sit there and do homework!" She giggles. "Or talk."

"Really." My mouth pinches.

She can't stop talking about the small classes where the tables are in a circle, the cafeteria with four entrees! Her super-cool English teacher who took them outside to sit on the grass and read poetry out loud. If you need to go to the bathroom, you just say so and don't need a wooden pass.

The story about our day is dying in my throat. I think about our new cafeteria. I got a baloney sandwich and a milk carton.

Francesca breathes: everything is *beautiful, great, amazing*. She leans closer, her hair falling across her cheek. "But here's the best part. An older kid is paired with you to show you around. So I was paired with this girl, Clarissa. But you know what happened?"

"What?" Josie smiles.

"Her twin came along! Evan. And oh my god, he is the cutest. They're from England too! We got to talking. Do you know he already knows what he wants to be?"

"What?" I ask.

"An archaeologist! He says next year when he goes to

high school, he may even get to go on a dig! He is . . . so beautiful." She clutches her hands around her knees.

Jealousy is pulsing in me. Josie gets quiet. Should I say something about John? That he has a nice smile? That he showed me to my room without it even being a school program?

"So what about you guys?"

Josie and I look at each other and shrug, Josie biting her lower lip. There's a wetness behind her eyes, making them glossy and big. "It's different."

"Kind of . . . crowded," I say.

I want to say more, but something isn't right with Josie. There's always a stillness to her that usually makes me feel calm. Still waters run deep, my father says. But she seems quieter than usual.

"I'm jealous," Francesca says. "You guys get to be together."

Josie and I look at each other and giggle. "I guess," I say. "If you count sitting in a cafeteria and drinking gross milk."

"And listening to Lucy Nelson be nasty," Josie adds. "I bet you don't miss that."

"No," Francesca says. But her voice has gone small.

Downstairs someone turns on the stereo, really loud. "Bloody hell!" Mrs. George shouts. "How many promises is that now?" A door slams.

I look over to the window, where I can hear a car roaring out of the driveway. Mr. George's convertible. When

I turn back, Francesca's mouth is crimped to the side. I wish I could reach over and smooth her face back to happy again.

* * *

At dinner, Mom announces that in a few weeks we have to go see Grandpa Joe for his birthday. Then she explains that some of the families are dropping out of the public schools and going to Catholic school. Then Karim and Daddy get into an argument about that, which annoys me. It's my school! But that's Karim: he's got a shock of black hair that he shakes back from his forehead, and always looks ready for a fight. "All you have to do is lower your head, mind your own business, and do your maths," Daddy says. Karim and I exchange glances. That's Daddy's answer for everything!

"Dad, that's not good enough anymore. It's not about being the exception. It's about being fair."

"Listen," my mother says. "No talking about the school with my family when we go for Grandpa Joe's birthday."

"Do I have to go?" Karim groans.

"Of course you do." She hands him a plate heaped with broiled potatoes, his favorite. "And you'll be polite. Don't take the bait."

Karim stabs at his potatoes.

"Promise?"

Karim lets loose a small smile. I know Karim's as loyal as they come. Especially to Mom, who he thinks got a

41

bad deal from her family. He just needs to mouth off now and then, call things "ridiculous" or "idiotic," like a tennis player taking swipes with his racket. And he's especially loyal to the three of us. That's what it means to be in our family. We're all we have.

*   *   *

After dinner, as I'm helping clear the dishes, my mother pulls me aside in the kitchen. "I want you to know something." She hesitates. "Regina said they didn't put Josie in SP."

There's a prickling under my skin. "What do you mean?"

"She's in the regular classes."

So that's what's been going on with Josie! Why she was so quiet at Francesca's. "It must be a mistake!"

"They're not sure. She took the test, like all of you, and we assumed—"

"But that's not right! Josie's smart! So smart!"

"Regina's going to talk to them." My mother turns back to the sink and twists on the faucet. "Don't bring it up unless Josie does. She must be very upset."

Walking back upstairs, I feel like my legs are made of heavy iron. We were always the special kids. Ever since we were picked after first grade to be in the gifted classes, we were the ones the teachers boasted about. When our test scores came back, our fifth grade teacher would call out, "I've got ten kids who are at a tenth grade reading level!

One is eleventh!" Josie wasn't always in my class, but she was always in the program.

She took in things carefully, slowly. When we'd sit in the school library, she'd pull her chair tight up to the table, and set a wrist on either side of her opened book. She'd go through each page, sometimes silently mouthing the words. One time the librarian hovered over us and whispered, "Honey, maybe you should try this instead." She set down a book with a skinny spine and big print. Josie dipped her head down. I saw the shame in her eyes. I snatched the new book away and put it back on the revolving shelf, even though the librarian glared at me. I didn't care.

There has to be a way. I have to get Josie into SP. Back with me.

CHAPTER 6

SASHAY

Over the next few days, Karim's words clang in my head. It's like I'm seeing JHS 241 through different eyes. All those big ideas I heard from the grown-ups: *Integration. Desegregation. Experiment.* Now when I look around me, this school doesn't feel brand-new. After each class, when the bell lets out its long bleat and everyone explodes into the halls—kids calling, "Hey, girl!"; teachers hollering, "Move along, folks, move along!"—it's like there are two schools here. The SP kids only flow into everyone else in the halls or the cafeteria, or for the elective classes.

Every day, Josie doesn't show up to the bus stop until the last minute. Her eyes look a little puffy and her mouth is turned down. She says she woke up late but I don't believe her. Josie's the type of person who sets out her clothes the night before and double- and triple-checks her books. I'm dying to ask her about SP, but Mom made me swear not to.

We don't even have our elective together. The gym wasn't ready, so they put us all in the auditorium for a special assembly. I only see Josie at lunch. We find a little corner in the noisy cafeteria, where she sits beside me, sipping her milk and spooning her Jell-O from its cup. She doesn't talk much. Not that it's easy to hear anyway. Josie keeps her shoulders tucked in, flinching. Three boys stand on a cafeteria bench and lob crumpled napkins at a group of girls. They shriek, laughing.

Josie is quieter than usual. She's wearing a button-up blouse, the kind that she usually wears to church, and a pleated skirt and high socks. Totally unfashionable.

"Girls and boys out!" the lunch aides yell, then fling open the doors, and kids go pouring outside.

Josie and I stare at each other. "Where do you want to go?" I ask.

"I don't know." She looks as bewildered as I feel.

"Take a walk?"

She nods.

We stroll by the handball courts, where the Spanish-speaking girls sit against the fence, flicking their long black hair, and watching boys slam balls against a concrete wall. Next come the basketball hoops, where the tallest and loudest boys play pickup or shout from the sides, elbows out near their hips. Clutches of other girls saunter in groups, cutting us up with their eyes. The girls from our old school are leaned up against a wall, but Josie doesn't want to hang with them either.

I lean a little closer. "I wonder if I'll see John today."

She jerks around and stops. "I don't want to talk to those boys again."

I blink. "Whatever."

"I mean it!"

We walk in silence. Not the old kind of silence but a new one.

* * *

For my last period on Friday, I make my way to dance class. The room is beautiful: the size of three classrooms, with floors that gleam like honey. A barre runs the length of the big windows and there's a dizzying wall of mirrors on the opposite side. Most girls here aren't in the SP classes. They're sitting cross-legged on the floor chatting, joshing each other. Some are already changed into leotards and tights. How did they know to do that?

"Ladies, ladies, enough!"

A short man is barreling into the middle of the room. "This is a class where you don't *talk*. You *do*!"

Mr. Sloan talks so fast, I have trouble following. We all line up against the mirror, smoothing our hair or checking our lip gloss. Then he shows us a move he calls a *sashay*. Each one of us has to do it across that polished floor. When I try the move, my arms are awkward and I jerk from side to side. Mr. Sloan is not impressed.

"Okay, girls, let me give it to you straight. I expect every one of you to get here on time, fully dressed. On dance days, there's no time to change in the bathroom. You wear your leotards underneath, *capisce?*"

We nod.

"I'm the father of three girls, so I know how long you take to get ready in the bathroom. My classroom you're ready to move the minute we start, *capisce?*"

"Mr. Sloan?"

Johanna steps into the room. She's changed into a maroon scoop-necked leotard. "I'm so sorry, but the girl's bathroom on the second floor was locked. I had to fetch a teacher." The word *fetch* is the way my dad speaks, Caribbean.

"Johanna!" he says with a broad smile. How does he know her? "Go ahead, show them how a sashay is done."

Johanna glides across the floor. Her muscles ripple, her arms float in the air, her chin is tipped, just so. Mr. Sloan looks like he's in love with her.

*   *   *

When the bell rings, I go down the wrong stairwell. I try to shove my way back up, but I'm pushed back by the wave of kids running down. I want to crawl into the corner and bawl my eyes out.

Then I hear someone call and see them elbow toward me. "Yo." John stops, sneakers squeaking.

I feel my mouth break into a smile. "Hi."

47

Today he's wearing belted pants that are a little too short. "You lost again?"

"Yes." I try to hide how embarrassed I am. "I'm trying to get outside. I've got to make the bus."

"You want me to take you?"

I pull my shoulders up. "I can do it."

"Come on. It's just this way." He leads me down a flight of stairs and then another.

"That bus ride long?" he asks.

"Yeah."

"Too bad. I live three blocks away."

I want to ask him a million things. Like, does he live in an apartment or a house? Does he have a brother or sister?

We step through a door into the warm sunshine where everyone's milling outside. Two girls who are nearby call, "Hey, John! Who you talking to?"

"No one."

I give him a glare. I'm no one? I start to push past him toward the bus line.

"Come on, John," a girl says. "We gotta go." She puts her hand around his arm. She's got long shiny fingernails. Before she leaves, the girl does a swivel and says to me, "You stop following him, you got that?"

John gently shakes her off. "None of that, Tanisha." He turns to me. "See you." Then he melts into a group of kids who scatter down the block. I can't move. Part of my body is walking down the street with them.

"Who was that?" Lucy Nelson asks as I join the line that's snaking toward the bus.

My neck feels warm. "Nobody."

She peers at me, skeptical. "Is that the boy who helped you?" Lucy is a lot bigger than me, with a round face and stubborn eyes. In a weird way, I'm impressed with her bluntness. The other girls glance at each other as we troop down the aisle and take our seats.

I can't believe I kept my mouth shut. One of my old teachers used to laughingly call me Miss But, for all the times my hand would jab the air, objecting in class. As I take my seat, I feel like a little worm. Not someone who can sashay across this school. How did I get so small, with no voice? When am I ever going to speak up again?

CHAPTER 7

THE BOYS ON THE CORNER

On Saturday I wake up in a better mood. Finally we can catch up with Francesca. I'm stuffed with stories and questions. What happened with that boy Evan? And maybe I can tell her about John. And maybe—just maybe— Josie will talk about her classes and we can put our heads together to get her back in SP. I already told Francesca about the situation the other night on the phone and she's mad too.

On Saturdays me and Francesca and Josie usually go to Patty's, the luncheonette. We sit on the vinyl stools, legs dangling, and eat scrambled eggs and triangle toast soaked in butter. The whole time we page through the Betty and Veronica comics from the rotating stand.

When Francesca's mother opens the door, her hair is

mussed to one side, and I can see her lingerie top peeking out beneath her robe. Her cigarette ash is quivering and long. Then I notice that Mr. George's car is not in the driveway. Francesca comes pounding down the stairs, pushing past her mother, who wavers in the background like a bowling pin that got knocked. "Can you get some milk?"

"Yeah, sure."

Francesca does an eye-roll to us and then stomps down the path, bending once to fling the newspaper onto their stoop. One week of seventh grade and Francesca has already become a teenager. She's dressed in cutoffs and a shirt that she's knotted at her belly button.

"Okay, spill," she declares, once we've settled on our stools and ordered our eggs.

I smile, testing my little straw with my teeth. I'm going to wait on John.

Josie shrugs. "Nothing much."

"My math teacher played the guitar while we did our equations," I tell Francesca.

"That's great!" Francesca says. "So I'm just hanging and trying to do my biology homework, when Evan plops down on the beanbag right next to me and asks if I play tennis."

"You don't," I say.

Now Francesca tilts close. "Just before he leaves, he says he hopes I'll come watch."

"Were his friends there too?" Josie suddenly asks.

I whirl around on my stool. I almost forgot she was there. Her face has gone still, the way it does sometimes.

"Yeah, I guess." Francesca sounds flustered. "Standing by the door, like always. He knows a lot of people. Why do you ask?"

Josie shrugs. "No reason."

I'm dying to ask Josie more. Just then our eggs and toast arrive. I'm ravenous, and after stuffing myself, I blurt out, "I like someone too." Before I know it, I've told her about John, not that there's that much. "He has a friend," I add. "Darren. He likes Josie."

"Ooh!" Francesca squeals. "Doubles!"

Josie hunches over her Coke, mouth tight. She's furious at me. Sliding off the stool, she mumbles, "I gotta go. I told my mom I'd help her today." Then she throws down her money and is out the door.

Me and Francesca look at each other. "I want to help her," I say. "The whole SP thing. But I don't know what to do."

"You've got to find out who can help," Francesca declares. "That's what my dad did. When he was little, his mom worked for some rich people. And he would go over there and ask a million questions about all their paintings and furniture."

These are the stories we've grown up with: How my dad walked five miles to school. How Mr. George had his college education paid for by that family. But we were the ones who weren't supposed to struggle like they did. We had skating parties and our own rooms and fluffy pillows that matched our quilts. We can buy as many books as we want from the Scholastic Book Club. I never thought a story like that had anything to do with us.

* * *

When Francesca and I step out of the luncheonette, something feels different. The air turns electric. Then we see them: a group of boys hanging on the corner, their eyes on our legs, our arms. I suddenly wish Francesca wasn't wearing cutoffs.

"Whoo, baby," one boy calls.

"Caramel," says another, and they elbow each other.

I want to disappear. But Francesca thrusts back her shoulders, flounces her hair.

The boys' eyes flash. This is better than they expected. One of them inches a little closer. "You from around here?"

"Could be."

I yank her by the elbow, steering her away and up the block. "Stay away from those boys."

She shakes me off. "They were just joking, Jamila."

"It wasn't funny."

Our Saturday reunion was nothing like I expected. No giggling or talking so much that you go from breakfast to

Francesca's room. Or to the playground swings, pushing our knees deep into the warm air.

Now I remind her, "The milk? For your mom?"

As I watch her march off to Key Food, what makes me so mad is Francesca can be so right and wrong at the same time.

CHAPTER 8

BEAUTIFUL

It's the second week, and I still haven't talked to Josie about SP. She's on strike. She won't sit on our bench in the yard. She doesn't talk to me on the bus. After school, she usually says she has to help her mother, though she never says what that is. The only thing I have to look forward to is seeing John—either at lunchtime when we give each other shy looks in the yard, or after school when I dawdle by the steps, hoping to spot him.

Finally it's Thursday, my first chance to be with Josie for Community Circle. But Josie is nowhere to be found among the kids chucking off their shoes on the new shiny floor.

"Come on in!" Miss Griffith greets me. She's the one who got up on the stage the first day of school. Her hair is a frizzy black cloud. Her eyes sparkle and she's again wearing silver bangles that slide up and down as she waves her arms. "Go on, take your shoes off, and take a seat in the circle. Everyone make room!"

When I sit down I spread my hand on the floor to my side to show the place is saved for Josie, but Lucy plunks down right next to me. Then I see Darren and Tanisha and another girl. They are right opposite me, Tanisha giving me cutting eyes. Cheeks burning, I stare at my crossed feet.

"Hey, Teach," Darren calls, grinning.

"Hey."

I flush, knowing he's John's friend.

Miss Griffith steps into the center of the circle and smiles. "Do you guys remember the strike when schools were closed?"

"Oh yeah!"

"I watched a lot of TV."

"I had to babysit my little brother!"

Miss Griffith laughs. "Well, I helped run a special school. We had something called open classrooms."

"What's that?"

"You could sit anywhere, really. In the hall if you liked."

Darren half-jumps up in a jaunty crouch. "See ya!"

We all look to see if Miss Griffith is going to get mad. But she smiles, with those twinkling eyes. "If it were up to me, I'd say fine. Children shouldn't be hemmed in. Learning is about roaming free with your mind and body."

Some kids nod, confused. She talks to us as if we're

grown-ups. "So you know that our bodies and minds are connected, right?" She explains that this is the one time when we can all *feel ourselves as a community.* Darren's mouth curls. He nudges Tanisha. I stop smiling. I like Miss Griffith, but I don't want to seem like a teacher's pet. Not in this school.

"Okay, enough with this boring talk! It's time to move! We're doing the Trust Game!"

Miss Griffith tells us to make a circle around her. We giggle and shove but manage to do it. "Now we need two people to stand in the middle. One of you shuts their eyes and leans backward until they're caught by the other person." She shuts her eyes and starts to tilt backward. "It means you have to be both trustworthy and trustful."

But nobody wants to be the person who trusts. So Miss Griffith breaks us up for our first try into girls and boys. I wind up in a circle with Tanisha.

"Go on, Jamila," she says. "You lean back."

"That's okay. You can go."

"No, you do it." She steps into the middle. "You so skinny. Not hard to catch you." Her voice has a funny edge.

I don't want to, but I take a step forward. I shut my eyes. I can hear Miss Griffith's voice, soft and nice. "Turn your shoulders, your arms to putty."

It takes a few tries. I keep not letting go and stumble back on my heels. "Come on!" the others cry. "Just trust!"

I let my spine soften. My head lolls back. Their breaths tickle my hair and I'm sinking into the warm cups of their

57

hands. Then there's a scrape of fingernails and nothing. I try to jerk up—too late. I'm sprawled on the polished wood floor, my elbow throbbing.

"Hon, are you okay?" Miss Griffith is crouched right next to me. She smells of some kind of spicy-sweet perfume. She called me *hon.* I almost cry.

"I'm fine." I rub the bone.

"What happened?"

I shake my head. "I don't know."

Miss Griffith stands and twirls. "Anyone know?"

"Lost her balance," Tanisha says.

Miss Griffith looks puzzled. "Must be the new floors. Be careful, kids."

But I know Tanisha let me go on purpose.

* * *

The bell sounds out and everyone scrambles to their feet, grabbing their books and bags, putting on their shoes. As I'm pushing through the door, Darren sidles up. "Hey, Teach! Wait up!"

"Hi." I keep walking. I'm in no mood to talk to him. Not after what Tanisha did.

"Come on! You don't have any time for me?"

I turn. "My name is Jamila."

He smiles. "Sorry." He asks, "Where's your friend? I thought she was in this Community thing?"

"I guess not."

"I see her at lunch but she don't say hi to me."

I shrug.

"Why don't she say hi?"

"I don't know. Maybe she doesn't remember you."

He grins. "She remembers me."

Reaching into his pocket, he hands me a note. It's been folded into a tiny square. "You give that to your friend?"

"She has a name."

"I know." He whispers, "Josie. Josefina."

I take the note, startled by the way he says Josie's name: soft and quiet. His shiny brown eyes are uncertain.

*   *   *

When I give Josie the note on the bus later, her mouth pinches tight and she twists around to read it, wedging her bag against the window.

"What's it say?"

She doesn't answer at first. "He wants to go out."

A slippery sensation wriggles down my chest. I don't know if it's because it's Darren doing the asking or because it's Josie who is officially being asked out by a boy. The first of us.

The bus pauses at a light and the traffic is at a standstill. The windows are glazed hot with sun. It's going to be a slow ride. Another thing they didn't tell us about busing: how long and boring the rides are.

"What are you going to say? You have to say something."

She keeps looking out the window at a sad-looking line of stores. Two of them are boarded up.

"Why?"

I'm astonished. A boy has given her a note! This is huge. "He gave it to me," I say. "He expects an answer." Of course, I know no such thing. But this is our chance. I can almost see the two of us sashaying down the hall, she with Darren and me with John.

"Maybe next week."

She folds the note back along its creases, slides it inside a notebook. For once, Josie's careful ways annoy me.

"Where were you, anyway? I thought you had Community Circle."

"I had to go somewhere." She fiddles with her rubber book strap. "Guidance."

I feel as if I'm going to explode any minute, yell at her for being so closemouthed. But with Josie you just have to stay quiet and wait. Let her find her own way.

"They gave me a test," she finally says. "To see about my reading."

"What about your reading?" I cry. "It's fine!"

Josie hesitates and then says, "Look, Jamila. I'm not like you and Francesca. I don't want . . ." This time, when she turns back around, she gives me her full-on back.

If anyone had told me this was what being in junior high would be like: Your best friend is silent beside you. You're skinny and knock-kneed and you get lost easily. You aren't at the top of the Ferris wheel.

I'd have said: You can have it.

* * *

The next Thursday in Community Circle, the door swings open and Josie comes sliding across the polished floor and drops down cross-legged, next to me. My heart leaps. We're together again for fifty-two whole minutes! Even though the girls on the other side of the circle keep nudging each other and whispering. Today Miss Griffith teaches us how to close our eyes and meditate and watch our thoughts move past "like clouds in the sky." Mostly, I keep sneaking glances at Josie. When we finish, those other girls cluster around.

"Where you from?" one girl asks Josie. Her bangs are curled stiff on her forehead, like she'd put an index finger inside and hair-sprayed the strands down. "How come you from that other school?"

Josie shrugs. "I live near there."

"Where's your mama from?"

"Jamaica."

The girl gives a firm nod. "Your daddy?"

"PR."

"You speak Spanish?"

"A little."

"What about you?" They swivel to stare at me. Funny that no one cared to know much about me before.

"My dad's—"

But Tanisha interrupts me. "You like Darren?" she

61

asks Josie. Tanisha is slender and sharp-boned, with a high slant to her cheeks. "He asked you to go out."

Nothing like getting to the point.

Josie blushes. She's plucking imaginary dust from the pleats of her skirt. Today she's got on old-fashioned white socks with pink roses trailing up the sides.

Just then the bell bleats. "Gotta go!" She grabs her shoes and rushes out the door. I'm not far behind.

*   *   *

On the bus, it's like the hurts that have been inside Josie come tumbling out. She tells me, "Two of those girls from Community Circle are in my homeroom. They sit on the other side of the room, but they keep staring at me."

"Why?"

She shrugs. "Maybe my name. Our homeroom teacher is so dumb. She can't get any of the names straight."

And then she tells me about her first weeks: How two boys broke into a fight in the back of the room. In math one day they called the security guard and pulled a kid out. Sometimes the room is so noisy she can't hear herself think. "I just want to get out."

"You have to!"

"But I can't be with you and everyone else in SP. They think I'm dumb! Everyone, all of them, they look at me and they say, she's with the dumb kids!"

"No, no!" I cry. "You're smart! You're so smart! Didn't your parents talk to them about SP?"

"They said no."

I'm stabbed. Josie tips her head, sobbing, hard. Her shoulders are rounded and shaking.

I reach out and touch her lightly. I'm so angry. I hate this school, splitting us up like this.

I whisper, "You are not dumb. Not ever." Then I reach for her hand. Her fingers twist into mine. "I'm going to figure out a way to fix this."

* * *

"Let's go sit in the yard," Josie says the next day. Something changed after talking the day before. Her eyes are sweet again. She's wearing her orange construction boots and, like me, a bandana is tied around her neck. Hers is blue and mine is red. We're back, the same, connected by that secret link. No matter where the school puts us.

We eat our grilled cheese the same way: nibbling the crust, then scarfing down the gooey middle. We wipe our mouths and then we start to walk. A slow circle around the yard. That's what we do best, me and Josie. Our elbows, arms touching. We leave the girls from our old school clumped in a corner, chatting. Past the churned-up pit left by the tractor, around to the handball courts where boys are smacking balls hard against the wall. A chain of girls sit against the fence. I hear bits of Spanglish, girls flipping their long hair, their halters showing strong, brown arms. A few nods. Next we're on to the basketball courts, where it's loud and the rim rattles.

We sit on our own bench. It's as if the air has been rinsed out, leaving it sparkling cool.

"Josie, I'm going to find a way to get you into SP."

She blinks a few times. "You can't do that." But her voice is warm.

"Watch me."

As we're talking, a group of girls stroll toward us. I sit up. It's the ones from the library and Community Circle. But no Tanisha, so I can breathe. They nudge each other, whispering, as they come closer.

"Hey," one says.

"Hey," Josie returns.

This girl wears a gray T-shirt that shows the straps of her bra. She looks years older than us. "You wanna come watch handball? We're cheering for Carlos."

I can feel Josie unfold, just a bit. She inches to the edge of the bench. The girls look right through me, like I'm invisible.

"Come on."

Josie looks at me helplessly. There's a hard hurt in my throat. But I'm glad for her too. She seems happier than I've seen her in weeks. Not so ashamed.

I brush her finger with mine. "Go on," I whisper. "I just want to stay here."

Grateful, she pushes up from the bench.

"See you on the bus," I say.

"Yeah," she says. "See you."

* * *

My lids sting. I watch Josie slip to the other side. Now she's in the center of a circle of girls. She's found her spot in the yard.

I keep my eyes on the basketball courts, then move them over to a corner where the girls from our old school chat. I could talk to them—Jill and Lucy would like it if I came over. But in a weird way, I want to be here, on this bench, feeling the hot, lost space where Josie was.

A commotion starts up a few feet away—shrieking boys and girls chase each other. "You gonna get it! Yeah, right!" They make figure eights around the yard. Two boys split off and run my way: John and Darren. John's got a grin as wide as anything.

My insides are lit up, blazing red.

He leans close and gives a tug on the bandana around my neck. It slides off easily.

"Hey, beautiful," he whispers.

It's like a leaf has twirled out of me, gold and flickering. I laugh as I jump up from the bench, running after John, who is waving the bandana. I may not be grown up like Johanna or sexy like Francesca or Spanish-special like Josie. But as I chase John to catch my bandana, I know two things: I am going to get Josie into SP.

And I am beautiful.

PART 2

CHAPTER 9

COWBOY

John and I start talking on the phone almost every night.

It's one month into seventh grade. Every morning me and Josie talk, but never about her and SP. It's not like I've come up with any great ideas anyway. Josie has made friends with Angela, who's in her homeroom, and I see them a lot, chatting in the halls or going over to the handball courts. Jill Siegel has made two new friends: Lonnie and Ronnie, twins who live in the neighborhood by the school. Jill tells me proudly, "They're geniuses." Ronnie wants to be a veterinarian and Lonnie an entomologist. I have to look that up—bugs. Lonnie wants to study bugs! Jill seems happy, though. She and the twins walk together in the hall and do study hall in the library, whispering excitedly about their math equations.

John and I don't have any classes together, not even

electives. We see each other at lunchtime but there are always too many other kids around. Sometimes we see each other in the halls and say hi, but we don't touch, not even our fingertips. Lucy Nelson is always bugging me about him. "Is he your boyfriend?" she asks on the bus. "Have you kissed him?"

"Not yet," I tell her.

"Well, my parents would never let me go out with a black boy."

"Lucy!" Jill wails. "That's mean!"

I've gone numb. Tears sting my eyes. What about *my* dad? Instead I say, "You don't know anything. He's great."

The bus ride is feeling longer and longer. Forty minutes, sometimes an hour, on a bus each way scoops out so much of my life. When I come home, I have to lie on my bed for half an hour, feeling the day ease from me like a groggy dream. Then I check the window to see if Josie or Francesca are around. If it's warm, we go to Carvel, lick the soft swirl ice cream and walk slowly home, letting the neighborhood wash back to us.

But the best is when, just as my mom is clearing the dinner table, the phone rings. She gives me her pale-eyed, skeptical look. The first few times John must have introduced himself, very politely, because Karim starts saying, "Yee-haw, it's the cowboy!"

I punch his arm, drag the red phone from the hall, and sit on the floor in my room, back against the door. That's as far as it reaches, the curly cord stretched tight. We can talk a good hour. I learn that John's mom is a nurse who works all the time on crazy shifts, and his dad works at the post office and is from South Carolina. They live with his grandmother, and he has an older brother in the army, Ronald, who he misses a lot.

John is in the other three-year SP. One night he tells me that he's the only black boy in his class. "Does that make you feel . . . weird?" I ask.

"I guess. I don't think about it much."

I don't believe him. He tells me that if he didn't do well in school, Nana, his grandmother, would swat him on the back of his head. He doesn't have a choice. I smile to myself. Daddy doesn't swat, but he doesn't give me and Karim a choice, either.

"I wish I could get Josie in there," I say.

"Why do you have to fix everything?" he asks.

I feel my jaw go tight. "I just do."

"Give it time. If she works hard, they'll notice and move her."

I want to believe him, but Karim has filled me with all kinds of ideas about "the system" and "oppression." And I'm impatient too. "Besides," I say, "I just want to be with Josie. That's the way it always was."

"That's nice."

I feel better. That's what John does. He's calm, always believes the best about people. And I burn to change things, especially the big things that seem so wrong. Josie not in SP. The feeling that we're not one school, or one community, like the cheery signs or speeches say.

*   *   *

The next day it's raining, so we have study hall in the library instead of recess. I jump at the chance to join Josie and her friend Angela to sit at one of the big tables. Darren strolls in and tells me John's out sick today. Then he acts goofy, trying to get Josie's attention. She keeps her eyes on her math textbook.

"You like that stuff?" His voice is soft.

She looks up at him. "It's not my favorite," she says with a slow smile. "But I don't have a favorite yet."

After the librarian shoos Darren away for making too much noise, I notice that Josie's math book is red, but mine's green. The spine on hers says *Fundamentals* instead of *Introduction to Algebra*. When I start flipping through, I see the problems look babyish, like what we did last year, maybe even the year before in fifth grade.

"How come you're doing this?" I ask, tapping her math book. "You've learned this already."

"The teacher says a lot of the kids haven't done it yet. She says I can review." She slides the book from me and tucks it into her bag. "It doesn't matter."

But it does matter. It isn't like John says. If Josie is doing math one or two years behind me, then how is she ever going to be the same as me again? She can't catch up.

I sneak a look at the science textbook she put to the side and see it's also a different color, though it says *Biology* on the spine, like mine.

"Hey, Josie?"

I see Angela scowl. I don't care. I want her to know Josie is my friend from long ago. Outside school.

"What did you mean the other day—asking Francesca if that boy's friends were there?"

Josie considers, smoothing her page with the side of her palm. "She isn't respecting herself," she says quietly. "Francesca says the shiny things on the outside. But inside she feels kind of bad. You shouldn't get so mad at her."

How is it that Josie can put things together like that, and she's in the "slower" classes? "You shouldn't be doing that math," I say.

Angela leans forward. She's a pretty, pale-skinned girl with full lips. "Why do you have to bother her? She doesn't want to do that other stuff." She turns to Josie. "So, you're coming over today?"

Josie smiles. "I have a note."

Not going on the bus! That's our time. Even if we barely talk. When the bell rings, I dash out of the library. That way I don't have to watch the two of them walking out. Together.

*   *   *

That night, I tell John about what happened in the library. "Angela makes me so mad!" I say.

"You're just jealous. Josie's your main squeeze."

I laugh. "What kind of expression is that?"

He laughs too. "I don't know. Old-fashioned, I guess."

"It sure is!"

"Maybe you can get a note, like Josie? Stay after school?"

"Maybe."

For some reason, whenever I imagine hanging out with John, it's always with Josie and Francesca too. I see us stopping for drippy pizza slices and SweeTarts that crumble in our mouths. Even as it grows late I can see all of us walking under the streetlamps, feeling our legs and muscles stretch, growing into a new big-kid place.

But my parents don't let me take the public buses. They're nervous about this neighborhood, where the storefronts are scrawled with graffiti and there are burglaries. My father doesn't want me to have any boys in my life yet. "You stick to your studies," he says.

I hear the dishwasher swishing below. My mother talking to my father. He's sitting on the couch, finishing calculations for a new hospital that's being built in the Bronx where he's the head engineer. "Jamila, you do your homework?" she calls up to me.

"I gotta go," I tell John. But I don't want to.

"What are you doing this weekend?" he asks.

"Ugh. I have to go to my grandfather's. It's his birthday."

"He's family. That's good."

I make a face even though he can't see. "I guess."

"So you'll ask your parents?"

I shut my eyes. It's as if I can see where he is, as if he's right outside: his house, his skinny garden, his corner feel as real to me as my own neighborhood.

"We'll figure it out," I say softly before hanging up.

CHAPTER 10

SAME OLD

On Sunday my family stuffs into the car and heads off to Long Island. Daddy always told me that this part of New York State is just a spit of land, an ice age afterthought. That's why it's so flat—millions of years ago the glaciers left a thin finger that points into the ocean.

For me, Long Island is that place where my mother is from and my family can never be from.

Grandpa Joe is waiting for us in the living room, cracking pistachio nuts into a glass bowl, the TV on to a Mets game. He grunts when we walk in the door, though there's a wrinkly smile creasing his face. That's about as much as you ever get from him.

"How's tricks?" Daddy asks, sitting down. He's dressed in tan slacks and a button-up shirt, with thin black socks and Oxford shoes, the kind that he wears for work. Daddy never seems to have any weekend clothes. Grandpa Joe, on the other hand, has on his Mets sweatshirt and faded jeans.

"Same old."

"You hear your cousin Dorothy is moving?" Grandma Grace calls out. "She's had it with the city."

She and Aunt Lee are fixing dinner in the kitchen, while Karim is out back in the garage with Mom's brother, Uncle Joe, helping him with his car. That's the way it always is here: It's a small house, but everyone scatters to their corners. Only my mom doesn't know where to go. She paces the living room while I watch her from the edge of the sofa. Sometimes she sneaks out for a cigarette on the back steps, which I'm not supposed to know. Grandma Grace wants her in the kitchen with Aunt Lee, helping snip the string beans or mash potatoes, but after a few minutes it always gets tense and no one talks. I know that Aunt Lee wishes my mother would be less sharp and Mom thinks my aunt has no backbone. But she's grateful to Aunt Lee. "It's good my mother has Lee," my mother always says. "She's the daughter my mother really wants."

"You know that boy across the way? He shipped out." Grandpa Joe's eyes glitter at the back door, as if he's talking to Karim.

"Which one?"

"Navy."

We've had that talk many times, about the draft and

77

serving. Three boys on their block have gone into the military. Grandpa Joe was in World War II. One time Karim came here in his denim jacket, an embroidered peace sign over the pocket, and Grandpa Joe sent him out of the house, said he better take that off and come back in again if he wanted to visit. Poor Mom went pale.

For years Grandpa Joe refused to talk to Mom, until we were little and Grandma Grace called her up and said, "For goodness' sakes, come to Easter dinner!" But whenever we come here, it's like we're on probation: we slip up, say the wrong thing, Grandpa Joe could send us away again.

"Read about maybe another strike happening," Uncle Joe remarks at lunch. "You remember a couple years back, the kids were out of school for weeks?"

"It wasn't so bad," my mother says. "All the mothers got together and we did our own schools. The kids had a lot of fun. We even went on trips—"

"It was a mess," Grandpa Joe interrupts. There's one way to see things. His way.

"Whyn't you move out here?" Grandma Grace asks. "A few new houses are up for sale. School's a hop and a skip from here. Jamila can get on her bike."

My parents exchange glances. Karim winks at me.

"Buying this plot of land is the best thing we ever did," Grandpa Joe says. "The city's goin' to pot."

My mother stiffens. "The city is fine."

"Oh yeah? What about all headaches, the crime and strikes and graffiti? And now this school nonsense?"

"Animals," Uncle Joe mutters. Aunt Lee nudges her husband to keep it shut.

My parents would never move here. In Queens, Daddy can get on a bus or subway and go to Manhattan, get lost in the crowds. Whenever we walk around Grandpa and Grandma's town, my parents never hold hands, even though they usually do that a lot. I remember one woman at the deli where Grandma Grace sent me and Dad and Karim for cold cuts; she eyed us coldly and craned her neck when Karim went to the refrigerator for more beers. "You know you can't buy those," she'd said, even though it was obvious my dad was paying.

"We'll see how this school works out," Dad says.

"Jamila," my grandmother says brightly. "Any sweethearts yet?"

Grandma Grace was a real beauty when she was young. "You should have seen the suitors I had to kick out of the way!" Grandpa Joe often says. She was the best ballroom dancer, twirling lightly on her toes, and she still goes to the hairdresser every week, curling her hair into gold waves that show off her rosy skin.

I can feel a blush warming my neck. I keep hoping there will be a time when I can ask my mom about hanging out with John. Or maybe I'm too scared to ask.

Karim kicks my ankle. "Oh yeah. She's got a beau who's a cowboy."

"How's that?" Aunt Lee asks.

"His name is John Wayne."

"What do you know!" There are chuckles all around the table. I let out a breath of relief.

"He walk you home?" Grandma Grace asks. "That's how we got started until your grandpa wore out his shoes!"

My throat is dry wood. "No, he lives far away."

"He lives in Jamaica," Karim adds.

I glare at him. Karim is all about taking things head-on. I'm not, especially when I know people will disapprove.

Silence. They've figured it out: He's black. Grandma and Grandpa know all about the school plan from the newspaper.

My grandfather's frown grows deeper. Everything's spoiled for me. I'm angry that Karim let out my private business and angry that it should matter. And it doesn't make any sense. What about my daddy? Grandpa Joe's my only grandfather, and this is the only family I have since Daddy's mom, Grandma Rashida, died a long time ago. It's like hugging a stone. We can never tell the truth with them, not all the way. We can never be ourselves.

I give Karim a push as we're walking toward the car. "Stupid," I hiss.

"What?"

"You weren't supposed to say anything!"

"The truth hurts."

No, I want to say, *you hurt.* But I can't say that out loud.

The car is quiet on the way back. We're a boat, floating through a dark cold river, the air inside hushed, gathered warm around us. Times like these make me feel how alone we are. Just us four. I even stop being mad at Karim, since my brother is all I've got, even with his big mouth.

"I just hate the way they talk to you," my mother finally sighs.

"How's that?" Daddy watches the road.

"You have how many degrees? They don't give you any respect!"

"But degrees aren't what they respect."

"They don't show any interest in us, in your work. You're overseeing a whole hospital!"

My father laughs. "You think that matters?" He lifts a hand from the steering wheel and sets it on my mother's hand—his dark on her pale one. "Oh, darlin', when you going to learn: Most people never change. It's the world around them that changes."

*   *   *

The next morning, we are kind and soft with each other as we often are after visits to my mother's family. I find Mom at the table. A plate of steaming popovers is there too, the kind where you bang a cardboard tube and the dough puffs out in stretchy slabs. Daddy has already left for work.

I manage to ask, "Hey, Mom?"

"Hmm?" She peers into her compact as she glides on her lipstick.

"You think maybe I can stay after school sometime?"

"What for?"

"To hang around with some friends."

She clicks the lipstick tube shut. Her eyes click too, as if she knows what I'm asking. "You know we can't pick you up, Jamila. Your father isn't back until late and I don't drive. It's better for now that you take the bus and come right back."

"It's so unfair!" I make a big show of shoving my textbook into my bag and flinging it on the floor, before I plop down on a chair opposite her. "I need to make new friends! It's a new school."

"What about Josie?"

"What about her?"

"Isn't she your friend?"

This stings. I think about her and Angela walking out of the library the other day. How Francesca is so boy crazy at her fancy school. "She has her own friends," I say. "She even goes to their houses."

"I'm sorry. That must be hard." She sighs. "This school is supposed to bring everyone together. Instead it's splitting us apart. Just the other day I heard there's some kind of petition circulating among the parents."

My stomach hurts. I don't want to hear about all that grown-up talk. I just want to go to John's. And I want Josie back with me.

My mother reaches out her hand. "Listen, I've heard those phone calls."

"So?"

"It's no news to you that your father isn't ready for boys and all that."

I nod.

"What were you planning on doing?"

"Just walking around. Nothing bad! Why does it have to be so complicated?"

My mother nods. "I know. It shouldn't be so hard. When I was your age, Jimmy Falano walked me home from junior high almost every day. My father told him he might as well mow our lawn if he was going to wear out our front path so much."

"See?"

"Things need to settle down there. I'm hearing lots of stories about the school. Some of the girls have been harassed. A boy says someone took money from him."

"Do you think Grandpa Joe is right? About moving to the suburbs?"

"Oh, Jamila. Maybe some people can do it that way. We can't." She sets a hand against my cheek. "I'll talk to your father, I promise. The best thing now is for you to focus on your grades. He's so worried that this school won't be as good as the other one. If you do well in the first semester, I think he'll be more open. Just be good."

She pushes the popovers toward me. These are the best moments with Mom, like when I was little and I'd curl up against her on the couch, set my arm against hers. "When am I going to get freckles like you?" I'd ask. She'd stroke my skin. "You don't need them, silly." Now I slather my popover with jam and butter and when I'm done, I'm ready for school.

Be good. As I pick up my bag and head out the door, I do feel good, buoyed by the quiet in our car last night, away from a family that does not understand us. Waking to my mother with her popovers, her kind hand on my cheek. That's what carries me on my long, long bus ride.

CHAPTER 11

THE TROUBLE WITH MRS. MARKOWITZ

After that visit with my grandparents, I float through my classes, moody and out of sorts. I don't know where I fit in this school. I could hang out with the girls from my neighborhood, but I never did that by myself. It was always with Josie and Francesca. And other than Darren, nobody in the regular classes wants to be friends. As I was rushing out of SP homeroom, I heard a girl in the hall whisper, "Stuck-up."

I've started to scribble on the Subjective side of my journal, even doing little cartoons, some of them mean, about my teachers or the other kids. I write: *On the outside everyone is doing what we're told. We go to classes. On the inside I can hear how people don't agree. I can see it in their mouths and their eyes.*

I especially write about Mrs. Markowitz, my social studies teacher. I hate her stiff hair and her dull-penny eyes. In my journal I write: *Mrs. Markowitz is obsessed with her attendance book. Every day she checks who remembers their textbook, who is sitting up straight. And she gives out mimeograph sheets that I could answer in my sleep. Boring!*

Today Mrs. Markowitz hands out another one of her mimeographs. The first question is *Explain the Domino Theory.* Already I'm bored. I thought social studies was supposed to be like civics, where everyone debates and talks. Isn't that what they promised in our brand-new school with new ideas?

"Dominoes. You mean what they play in the park?" one boy calls out.

"My grandpa likes dominoes!" José laughs.

"You've heard about the Domino Theory," Mrs. Markowitz says. "If we don't stop Communism in Vietnam"—she points to the map hanging behind her and lets her hand sweep across the Pacific—"Australia will turn Red next!"

I poke my hand in the air. "Not true."

"What's not true?"

"That Australia will go next. And even President Nixon says we have to get out of the war."

"Moving on. Explain the Monroe Doctrine. . . ."

"Wait," I say. "We're not done."

"You're done, Jamila."

"But you said Australia will go Communist. How can you say that?"

"It's nearby, that's why."

"But it's a continent! It's not the same!"

I'm being obnoxious and I can't stop. Daddy always grilled me on geography. And mostly I'm just repeating what Karim says at the dinner table—how we're *killing babies in Vietnam.* How we are *imperialistic,* even though I don't know what that means.

"That's a demerit, Miss Clarke."

"But what you said was wrong—"

Johanna, who is sitting in front of me, twists around and hisses, "Will you just be quiet?"

Stunned, I sit back. Johanna smoothly turns. She seems a million years older than me. Johanna plans to run for class president. Sure enough, Mrs. Markowitz gives her a stack of paper to hand out to the rest of us. I feel a stab of jealousy.

Across the top it reads *How to Use Your Local Library.* "Every one of you is going to do a research paper," Mrs. Markowitz says.

"Seems pretty dumb," I mutter.

"That's enough!"

I tremble, but a smirk plays around my mouth.

Next thing I know, she's standing next to my desk and has snatched my journal.

"What's this?" She starts flipping pages and reading

out loud. "Mrs. Fine is pretty but she has thick ankles. The boys are so dumb in my class."

There's snickering all around. "Hey!" Joey calls out. "Who's dumb?"

"You are!" Lucy says.

"You can't do that!" I leap to take it back.

But she's reading more. About everything: My feelings about the school and all that's wrong. How I see the teachers. My face burns. Even Johanna is shaking her head in surprise.

I lunge and try to grab the notebook.

"Out!"

A few gasps behind me. Lucy Nelson makes a big O with her mouth.

"Go on, Miss Clarke. Take your bag, and go right down to Mrs. Johnson's office."

"But what about my journal?"

Smiling, she opens her desk drawer, tosses it in, and slams the drawer shut.

Numb, I gather up my stuff.

* * *

Mrs. Johnson sternly questions me about what happened.

"She took my journal! And read it out loud! That's only supposed to happen if you choose to read it to the class!"

Her eyebrows rise. "Did you show her disrespect?"

I sag. "I guess. Just stupid stuff."

88

In truth, I'm mad at everything. Mrs. Markowitz. And myself. I actually like the idea of going to the library. I'm just so angry and it was easier to mouth off.

"Yes, well, we don't do 'stupid stuff' in a class. We—" Before she can finish, there's a clamor outside. I hear a string of curses and the secretary pops her head in. "So sorry, but we've got this situation—"

Mrs. Johnson rises. Outside, Darren and two other boys are slumped on the bench. "Again, Darren?"

"Sorry, ma'am." When Darren sees me, though, he grins, whispering, "Hey, what are you doing here?"

"Social studies. I opened my big mouth."

"I bet."

Mrs. Johnson gives me a nudge. "That's enough, Miss Clarke. I'll have them write you a pass. This is a warning. Next time, we're looking at something more serious."

* * *

At lunch, I'm by myself. Josie is over by the handball courts with Angela. Darren comes to sit, buddy-style, on the shady bench. "Hey, Teach, you okay?"

"I guess."

"No fun getting sent to Mrs. Johnson."

I'm still pretty sore about earlier. But after what happened to me, I wonder about Darren. He's quick, always figuring things out: How to get out of phys ed without his sneakers. How to get a few more days on his biology homework. How to hit me up for fifty cents for a pizza

89

slice. Bad words flare from his mouth. Sometimes getting in trouble means you're bored. Or mad. And I wonder . . . maybe he's stuck on Josie to help him be someone different, to not get mad so easily.

"Will you do something for me?" I ask.

"What?"

"Tanisha . . . she's always giving me a hard time."

He throws back his head and laughs. "Yeah. She doesn't like John going with a white girl."

"But I'm not white."

"It's crazy. My aunt, she's whiter than you are." He shakes his head. "It's just because of where you live. She's got you pegged another way."

"And the girls in my neighborhood peg me another way too."

"You're not black or white. Nobody got a fix on that. In biology today we talked about species. You know that in some way we're related to dogs?" He shakes his head. "All kind of mix-ups in our genes and people go and scream about a light-skinned girl with straight or kinky hair. It's messed up."

I look at him. Darren's way smarter than he lets on, smarter than the boys I argue with in SP class. Today he's wearing the same worn-out gray T-shirt he had on yesterday and no jacket, even though there's a chill in the air. His elbows are ash-bony. John told me Darren lives with his mother in the attic of someone else's house. When I told him about how Darren's always hitting me up for money for food, John said, "That's because his mother can't cook a can of beans."

Now Darren says to me, "Don't you bother about Tanisha. She'll get over it. You've got to go fire with fire."

"What's that mean?"

"You've got to fight her. Then she'll respect you."

*   *   *

I push hard through the hallways, using my elbows. I'm already late to science. Out of a clump of girls, Tanisha surges forward, just inches from me. She looks model-pretty in a red sleeveless top that shows off her arms.

"Girl," she whispers, her breath fierce in my ear. "You stay with your own race."

I stop, rooted to the spot, heat crawling all over my face. I want to cry. None of what my parents say, the soft way they gather our family together and make us special, helps me now. I'm stuck, same as with Grandpa Joe. Same as when Lucy Nelson says her nasty words.

Stay with your own race, I think as I walk into class and slump down in my chair. What does that mean, anyway? What is "my own race"?

CHAPTER 12

SEVEN MINUTES
IN HEAVEN

"I need your help."

Francesca calls on Saturday. We don't get to see each other much during the week, since she always comes home late. "Can you come with me to the city?" she asks. "That's where Evan hangs out with his friends."

"Does he know you're coming?"

"Sort of."

I'm doubtful. But I'm glad Francesca is turning to me. Especially these days. Half an hour later I'm in the back seat of her dad's convertible, wind whipping our hair into knots as we clatter over the 59th Street Bridge, until we shriek so much that he agrees to put up the roof. As we pull up to the curb on the East Side, he gives Francesca a wad of cash, which she happily stuffs in her little pocket-book, twisting the lock shut. "See you later?" she asks.

"Baby, I got some stuff in the city. Don't know when I'll be back. You and your mother work out the pickup."

Her face drops for a moment. "Okay, Daddy."

And then he roars off, the roof folding back again as he weaves into traffic.

I've caught some of Francesca's fever. We trip down Madison Avenue, passing women with stiff shiny shopping bags and stores lit up like stages. I'm sure everyone must notice how grown up we are.

She points Evan out, sitting with his friends in a coffee shop: streaky blond-brown hair that waves down at the backs of his ears; a crumpled pink shirt, tail hanging out. When we slide into seats a few tables down with Cokes, his eyes graze over us, but he doesn't come over. There's another booth of girls, and they nudge each other as we walk in. Weirdly, every one of the kids has straight blond hair that they keep flicking off their shoulders. They wear white shorts and pastel polo shorts. Their tennis rackets lean against the side of the booths. I get a wobbly feeling. Does anyone look like Francesca at her school? Do they pick on her the way Tanisha picks on me?

When the other girls leave, flashing their braces-filled smiles, Francesca heads right over to Evan. "Hey," she calls.

"Francesca! Whoa. Didn't see you there. What brings you to our side of the woods?" I can hear his British accent. It reminds me of someone spinning their tennis racket.

"My dad. His shop isn't far."

Evan nods toward me. "That your friend?"

"Yeah." A flutter of panic. "This is Jamila."

They all nod, say hi, but I don't like the way their eyes trail up and down. Like the boys at Patty's but different, as if deciding whether to buy something or not.

"Where are you from?" Evan asks.

"Cedar Gardens. Across the street from Francesca's."

"No, I mean like *originally*?" Grinning, he bites into a floppy French fry.

People always ask that. Where are you from? I know what they mean. But I don't like giving them the whole story.

"Queens," I say.

His friends laugh.

"What're you laughing at?" I ask.

"Nothing," one of the boys answers. "Just never been there."

"Me neither," someone else says.

I can't help but feel they're making fun of me, of the whole borough.

"You wanna hang?"

I see an eye-slide between Evan and the other boys: Andy, Michael, and Tres. Soon we're on the street, trailing after them to Central Park, where we clamber up the big gray rocks, and Evan and his friends horse around, using their tennis rackets to swat balls that the others have to catch in the air. That's fun for a while, until Andy gets a turned ankle and we all flop down on the grass. Evan is sitting right up next to Francesca, so their legs are almost touching.

"Hey," Andy says. "Let's go to my place. I gotta put ice on this."

"Your parents home?"

"Nah. Catching the last of the season."

As we get up from the ground, I'm queasy. I tell myself this is what you do. You go to strange boys' apartments as if it's nothing. Isn't this what I want? By now Evan and Francesca are walking with each other. Not quite holding hands, but he gently knocks his shoulder into hers. She tilts her chin up and laughs.

*   *   *

The lobby is huge—flickering strands of gilt and bronze and marble; the elevator man greets all the boys by their first names. When the gates clatter open on Andy's floor, we're in a private hall. A table holds a large vase spurting long-stemmed orange flowers. A heavyset woman in a blue uniform with white collar greets us at the door. "You in for now?" She has a Jamaican accent. "Your parents say they're coming home five tomorrow."

"Thanks, Carlaina. We're just going to hang for a while."

As we troop past, she gives Francesca and me a wary, stern look, and I'm flooded with shame.

If this were any other time, I'd probably admire this place. White fluffy couches, blue-and-white porcelain lamps. But I'm seesawing with nervousness. Especially when I realize that everyone here is older than us—ninth grade. Francesca perches on the sofa edge next to Evan, smiling, one ankle bouncing.

Andy limps back into the room, holding a bag of ice, and plops down next to me. "Seven minutes in heaven!" he declares.

"But there's only two of us," I say, faltering.

"That's okay." He's already scrambling to find a bottle that he places on the rug.

The first spin is Tres and me. He looks just as embarrassed as I feel, a weak smile wobbling on his mouth. We get up and stand opposite each other in the hall. My arms are rigid at my sides. I don't want to do this. He gives me a hug and I pull back, quick. Inside is a sickening sensation, like I'm dropping too fast in an elevator. He seems relieved that it's over.

We spin the bottle a few more times, but every time, it stops on one of the boys, so they guffaw and yell. At one point Andy bumps into Francesca, and then he thrusts his arm out. "See?" Andy points out. "With my tan, we're almost the same."

"That's what's nice about halfies," Evan says.

"Exotic, yeah."

Francesca laughs but I wonder when we're going to

leave, when the bottle spins once more and lands on Evan and Francesca. "Figures!" Andy groans. They give each other knowing smiles. Her cheeks go pink.

"Just seven, remember!"

"Hah!" Evan laughs.

They scurry off to another room. It seems forever that they're gone, though it's probably just a few minutes, the rest of us smiling nervously or fiddling with the bottle until Michael and Tres go over to the TV and switch on a football game. Andy slides closer to me, his bag of ice forgotten. "You're pretty."

I just sit with my fingers tensed between my knees. "Hey, beautiful," John had said to me. What am I doing here? I can't believe Francesca left me like this.

"You don't think you're pretty?"

"I never really thought about it." Heat pinpricks my face. I jump up, furious. "Where's the bathroom?"

"Down the hall."

I march down a hall covered in a busy rose wallpaper until I find the bathroom. I sit on the toilet lid waiting for the tears to spill. They don't. I stare at the pictures of sailboats. I wash my hands, but then I'm embarrassed about wiping them on the perfect towels embroidered with big fat letters.

When I get back into the living room, Francesca is sitting on the floor, her face flushed. Evan has joined the other boys, over by the TV.

"I gotta go," I say through gritted teeth.

"Why?"

"Now." She can tell how angry I am. "How are we getting back, anyway?"

* * *

We call from the phone in the kitchen, and my parents are surprisingly easygoing when they hear neither of Francesca's parents are available and we have to take the subway and bus. I guess because I'm in a good neighborhood and with Francesca. When we settle down in our subway seats, she asks me, "Why did you do that? Make us leave?"

My chest burns. "It was getting late."

"Isn't Evan cute?"

"Yeah, but—" I hesitate. "Those weren't nice things he said. About being a halfie."

"Oh, come on, Jamila. He was just kidding."

But I don't think he was. Francesca looks smaller. Her frizzy hair has come out of its barrettes. Her full lips seem mashed up, bruised.

"You need to be careful."

"You're just jealous because I have a boyfriend."

I feel as if there's a fish bone stuck in my throat, I'm so angry. *Is he your boyfriend?* I want to ask. Because I noticed he didn't hold hands with her on the street. None of the other coffee shop girls were there. And he kissed her behind closed doors. It was just a game.

We don't talk for most of the subway ride, our legs jiggling next to each other, then on to the bus and walking the few blocks home. After my anger wears off, I'm hurt. It's as if I don't know Francesca anymore.

Just as we reach Francesca's gate, I say quietly, "You know, I do have a boyfriend."

She looks surprised. "Really?"

"We talk on the phone," I say. "Almost every night."

"Why didn't you tell me?" She sounds hurt. "It's so unfair. You and Josie know everything about each other."

"Not really," I say softly.

"Why haven't I seen him?"

I don't know how to answer. Why is it okay that my parents let me go all the way on the subway and bus to Manhattan and I can't even stay after school? "I'm going to his place to hang out soon."

"Cool." She seems genuinely excited. I feel bad for how angry I was before. She's just trying to fit in, like me, in a school that has no place for us. And it is worse for her. She really is on her own there among those girls and boys. She's more outside than we are.

*　*　*

Back at home I get it into my head: I have to see John after school. It's dumb just to talk on the phone. No wonder Francesca was surprised. So I plan it out: After dinner I hand my mother the sheet about the research paper.

99

Then I explain that I need to spend a few afternoons at the main library in Jamaica. Instead I'll go home with John. My mother squints as she reads the mimeograph.

"Don't you have any friends you can go with? Like Jill?"

"She's not in my class."

"No one else?"

"No."

My mother sighs. "Okay," she says. "But you get on that bus before it's dark."

CHAPTER 13

BEANS

Two days later, when I'm going to John's, I can't concentrate in class. I doodle all over my notebook, swirling the word *John* until it's covered in loops so no one can make fun of me. I try to catch sight of myself in a window reflection, noticing my secret smile. In dance class I'm so dreamy I find myself on the wrong side of the room from everyone else. "Miss Clarke, care to join us?" Mr. Sloan calls. Johanna glares at me, hands on her hips. We're starting on a new dance for a special assembly in the spring, and she leads.

Finally it's the end of the day and I'm bolting down the front steps. The kids from my neighborhood are streaming the other way.

"Where are you going?" Lucy calls.

"To a friend's house."

"Do you have a note?"

"Yes." I squirm because it's for the Jamaica Library. "Sort of."

"You can't do that."

"Do what?"

"Not take the bus."

"Watch me."

And then I saunter off, giddy, to John at the corner. He's wearing a white shirt and a cardigan with leather buttons. He looks like a miniature Dad.

We walk down the street, and more kids melt away, shouting, weaving between cars. It's a funny feeling: I don't stick out here the same way I do in my neighborhood.

Most of the houses are smaller and some have a concrete space in front, no grass. Pairs of high-top sneakers twist from the telephone wires. We pass a fried chicken place and a liquor store with a grate covering its windows so you can barely see the bottles inside.

At one house, a group of girls sits on the stoop. Two younger girls are jumping rope, making a flick-flick sound on the pavement. The older girls flap down cards on the steps.

"Hey, John," they call.

We pause, me stiff. I recognize a few of Tanisha's friends. "You hanging over here today?" one girl asks me.

"I am."

She gives me the once-over. "How come you live over in that other neighborhood?"

I shrug. "My parents like it."

"Let her go, man," John says. "She's okay."

The girl waves her hand. "We just kidding."

They return to their card game. We stop in a corner store for SweeTarts. The shopkeeper greets John and asks after John's brother, Ronald, how he's doing in the army. "We're praying he's staying safe," the man says. I love everything about this place: the light streaking down through the windows, the man slipping an extra packet of gum into John's hand. And then outside, a few more people wave from steps as we walk. Even with those girls and their questions poking me, I feel good. Here, with these faces that look like me, I can move like I belong.

* * *

John's house is a robin's egg blue, with a tidy yard in the front, rimmed by a metal fence. They have a grate over their door too, with two locks. Once inside, we're in a small, dark living room; all the furniture is sheathed in plastic. The curtains are drawn and there are porcelain horses gleaming on a shelf, along with pictures of John F. Kennedy and Martin Luther King Jr., and Ronald in a uniform, and John when he was young, missing his two front teeth. A Bible sits on a table, a pair of half-glasses resting on top. I flinch. My mom is an atheist and my dad

103

told me he had enough religion growing up, so he was done with it. Josie goes to church; even Francesca dresses up for holidays and attends services. It's just another way my family makes it harder for me.

An elderly woman patters down the stairs. A green smock dress drapes around her thin bones. She moves lightly into the room, like a dancer.

"Hey, Nana." John puts his book bag on the dining table.

"You know better than to put that there. And you going to introduce me to your friend?"

"This is Jamila Clarke."

"Pleased to meet you, ma'am," I say.

She smiles. "You like ginger cookies?"

When I nod, she goes to the cupboard, shakes some out of a plastic tub, and sets them on a plate for us. "I'm going to listen to my radio show. Nobody listens to radio anymore but I do." She wags her finger at John. "You go out, you make sure you lock the door. Lady down the street—they walked right into her place and took her knitting bag. What they going to do with that?"

"I don't know, Nana."

"Boys losing all sense of who they are."

And then she goes upstairs. John has a wide grin. "Nana has a lot of opinions."

We stare at each other, suddenly awkward. I feel a hot rush in my throat. After all these nights talking on the phone, what do we do? He leads me to the couch, his hand as moist as mine. We lean toward each other and try kissing for a while. It's better than giving Tres a hug, but not much more. The couch is slippery and hard, for one. And I can't get rid of the swampy feeling in my stomach. I lied to my parents. I'm not supposed to be here, even if his grandmother did give us ginger cookies.

But it's like I've passed a test: I've kissed my boyfriend in his house. It's a relief when we go outside on his front stoop. We sit together, knees touching, as he calls out to different kids or grown-ups that pass by. The sun starts tipping behind the buildings. The sky is aluminum gray. I can see another clump of sneakers, twisting on shoelaces.

"Jamila, best you get going soon," his grandmother calls from inside the house.

"Yes, ma'am." John sits up on the step, hands folded on his lap.

"Yes, ma'am," I say too.

"First you come out back and help me."

We go through the clapping screen door to the back, where there are flourishing rows of spindly plants—tomatoes in V-shaped stands and squashes plumping under their frilly leaves. Nana wanders in the rows and I help her snap off beans. "These are the last of the season," she explains, and drops them in a wrinkled paper bag, which she hands to me. "I grow them and everyone on this block says they better than what you get at Key Food."

"They are, Nana," John says.

I nod, smiling.

We sit on the back concrete steps, in the waning light, as his nana talks more. Since I never met my grandma Rashida, it's like I'm sitting next to her, with her ashy legs, her proud garden. I want to linger a little longer but Nana says, "Don't want it to be late when you get on the bus. Not around here. John, you stay with her until she gets on the bus, you understand?"

*   *   *

When I walk in the door, my mom is furious, clinking down silverware and glasses and plates—usually my job. "Do you know what time it is?"

"Yeah. Sorry. The bus was late."

"Late? Is that all you have to say?"

"I told you! I couldn't help it!"

"Didn't I tell you to come right home after the library?"

"I said I was sorry already! Will you get off my back?"

My mother tips back, surprised. I'm the good kid. I'm not Karim. But something about strolling down strange streets, holding hands, has given me a new strength. I'm a girl who gets on an evening bus. A girl with a boyfriend and secrets.

As I head upstairs, my mother asks, "How was your research?"

Her eyes are trailing up my legs. My mom's no dummy. She knows when I'm lying. "Okay."

"It's a big library. I hope you found what you needed."

"Yeah."

"You know, I was out of my mind with worry."

I pivot and stare down at her through the banister. "Why do you have to make such a big deal? Why is it so bad for me to hang there? It's just a place. I think you're prejudiced too! Just like all the people you complain about!"

My mother sets both her hands on her waist. "Is that right? Your father works twice as hard as every other engineer at his job so we can live in this neighborhood. This is where we want to raise you. The rent costs a fortune, do you know that?"

Shaking, I march up the stairs and bang my door shut.

I hate them. I hate that they fill me with all their grown-up problems.

I think of all the voices calling to us as we sat on John's stoop, his grandmother bending in the garden. Even after I hear my father come home, I stay in my room. And when it's time to come down to eat, I take out the wrinkled bag of beans. It smells of fresh earth and a touch of lavender, Nana's scent. I crunch down, relish the fresh taste. Then I tuck it away in the back of my desk drawer and go downstairs.

CHAPTER 14

———

FIGHT

Fourth period. I'm turning a corner when Tanisha strides toward me. "I saw you yesterday!" I can see her mouth open, but this time, before she has a chance to taunt me, I put up the flats of my hands and push, hard, against her shoulders. Her eyes pop open, showing her spiky lashes. Even as I do it, I'm surprised at how small and compact she is. She stumbles backward into a wall, shocked. It takes a moment for her to gather herself. Then she wipes her mouth and lunges toward me. My bag strap is tugged off my shoulder, my hair yanked. The air blurs as we let a few slaps fly.

"Oooh!" someone cries.

"Fight!"

The next thing I know, I'm being dragged away by

strong hands. Mrs. Johnson pulls us down the hall and deposits us in two seats in her office. She slams her door shut with a kick of her high heel.

"Can you explain what is going on?"

My heart is skipping so fast I can't even breathe. "You've got to fight her," Darren had told me. I thought I did what was needed. But the words stay stuck. Outside an announcement drones, the sound muffled. Behind the frosted glass the shapes of secretaries move back and forth. I'd give anything to be out there.

"We'll stay here for as long as it takes. You girls need to work it out."

Tanisha's head lifts. "You always hanging with John!"

I finger the strap on my bag. "So?"

"Why John have to go with a white girl?"

"I'm not white," I say in a quiet voice.

"I don't know what you are." She adds, "You with all the white kids."

Mrs. Johnson makes a bridge of her hands. "Tanisha, why does it matter?"

She doesn't answer. I can see her lip quiver, a shiny welling-up in her eyes.

"Jamila, do you have anything to say? If I understand correctly, you initiated the physical altercation."

I shake my head.

Finally, Tanisha speaks. "Maybe you not white, but you all come here and think you're better than us."

"That's not true." But somehow her words make my face burn. Is she right? Didn't our teachers at our old school always say we were special and smart?

Mrs. Johnson's face softens. "You girls probably have more in common than you realize."

Neither of us say anything.

"All right. We're done. I'll be contacting your parents."

I step into a loud, clanging world—lockers slamming, bells sounding out. My knees are shaky. I have nowhere to hide, nowhere to fit. Later, on the bus, as I make my way down the aisle, I feel all the other girls' eyes press on me. I can see what some think: I've gone over to the other side.

But then Josie is there, pressing my hand. "It'll be okay," she whispers.

* * *

"Suspended?" my father asks. "How can that be?"

"It's just a day."

"Suspended?" he repeats. He can't believe that word, fixed to me. We're in the living room, my dad on the couch, my mom with her elbows on the arms of the rocking chair, and me twisting in the center of the rug.

"The assistant principal said you've also been giving your social studies teacher some mouth."

I hang my head. "She's mean. She took my journal."

My parents look at each other. "There are always mean teachers. But you can't disrespect them," my mother says.

"I don't even understand about this fight. How could you even know each other enough?" my father asks.

"We don't know each other."

"Is Josie involved with this?" my mother asks.

"No." Everything goes tight inside me. "I told you, she has other friends." At least Josie sat with me on the bus. She didn't ask many questions or give me that weirded-out stare like the other girls.

"But you've got some business with this girl."

"She's been picking on me for weeks!" I cry. "All because of me and John being together." I can't help how it slips out of me. I want, and don't want, them to know. I have someone. A boy, all mine.

"John who?"

"The boy I talk on the phone with." I take a breath. "Then she saw us together."

"Where?"

I swallow. "The other day. I went to John's house and hung out in his neighborhood. Tanisha got mad when she saw us walking around."

They exchange glances. "So you lied to us."

My head droops. "Yes." *You made me lie,* I want to say.

The worst part about getting in trouble isn't what they say. It's seeing a flinch in my father's face. And my mother turning from me. I'm disappointed in everyone: all the adults at my stupid school, with their big bright words. They don't get how hard it is to fit in.

I go upstairs and sit at my desk, stare numbly out the window. Francesca's house is dark except for the porch light. Would she understand if I told her? Her school seems so different, with beanbag chairs and no hall passes. Then I slide open my drawer and see the crumpled bag of beans. The paper has damp spots and when I open it up, there's a musty smell, no more Nana-lavender scent. I take the bag, shove it deep down at the bottom of my garbage.

PART 3

CHAPTER 15

NEEDLE

The fall goes gray and brown. Leaves dwindle on the trees. Me and John can just catch each other here and there between classes. Most of the time I feel I'm hiding inside. Afraid to go out, afraid to be seen.

The bus ride feels longer. Maybe it's because I'm starting to notice that something bigger is going on in the city. Everyone is edgier, angry. You can feel it in the way people squint through the bus windows. The subway cars shuttling past in a smear of graffiti. Triple locks on our doors and no one leaves their bikes out anymore. Meanwhile, kids are expected to glide across neighborhoods and make the world right. It's supposed to be easy. But what about neighbors sitting on stoops, faces stony at the sight of us? Families who shut their curtains, switch on the TV, and mutter bad names. The ride is longer and rougher than anyone ever let on.

One evening just before we sit down at the table, the phone rings. Daddy answers. Clearly he doesn't like what he's hearing; he frowns, jots down some notes, then shoves the slip of paper into his pocket.

"Who was that?"

"Mr. Rowan." He pauses. "Tomorrow the parents are going to picket the board of ed."

"Are you going?" my mother asks.

"Of course not!" He takes the bowl of rice. "I may have my reservations but—"

"Reservations!" Karim spits out. "That's what you call them?"

"They do have a point," Daddy says. "There are problems. You saw what happened with Jamila. She's starting to act tough."

I wince.

"Daddy, it isn't like your day," Karim says. "When we could be that one family let in. Or the cute scholarship boy everyone feels good about. This is about the people."

"The people." My father smiles. "What do you know about the people?"

Furious, Karim bangs down his chair. Daddy and Karim are fighting a lot these days. That's because Karim wants to drop out of his high-level physics class and take shop. "You are not going to work with your hands!" Daddy told him. "I work all day with men who didn't

116

have half the chance you have. And here you want to throw it away?"

After dinner, Karim stalks off and locks himself in his bedroom, turning up his music so loud, I can barely concentrate on my homework. Secretly, I feel a little thrill, the way he stands up to Daddy.

That night I tell John about what my brother said at dinner. "I could never do that."

"Me neither," John agrees.

But some part of me wishes I could. That I knew how to stand up for something. For myself.

* * *

"You."

My stomach quivers. I'm standing at my locker and it is Mrs. Johnson in her three-inch heels. Why does she wear shoes like that when she is already so tall?

"Me?"

"Yes, you, come with me."

We walk briskly down the hall, me trailing behind her. What have I done? I've tried to be good, keep my mouth shut. With Mrs. Markowitz, I take lots of deep breaths and lower my eyes. I definitely steer clear of Tanisha and her crew.

"I've been thinking," Mrs. Johnson says, after we settle into her office. "You actually have some good energy. It just goes in all the wrong ways. Do you think that's true?"

I hang my head. "Probably."

"I've got an idea. Are you organized?"

"I think so."

"I bet you are. You're going to come work with me during your lunch break. Help out with office matters."

My heart sinks; that's the only time I get to see John.

"What's the matter? You don't want to do it?"

I squeeze the spine of my loose-leaf binder. "No, it's okay. Sure."

"Sure? Is that the proper way to address me?"

"No, ma'am."

She gives a broad smile. Today she's got on a fire engine–red suit and crimson heels. Mrs. Johnson once told me that she has so many shoes she took over all the closets in the other bedrooms in her house. "My husband always says, 'Who lives here—me or the shoes?'!" she said with a laugh.

"Excellent. I think you're a good girl, Jamila. Many of the teachers say you can be quite thoughtful. Miss Fine says she enjoyed what you shared in your Objective-Subjective notebook."

I'm about to spit out, *Then why can't I get my journal back?* when there's a loud rap on the door. Mrs. Johnson's head lifts up. Darren slumps into the room, stands uncertainly. Today his jeans hang stiff from his hips.

"What now, Darren?"

He mumbles something about a fight.

"Can you speak clearly? And stand up straight when you talk?" She nods to me. "Jamila, you can go now. Tell the secretary to give you a slip."

Our eyes flicker to each other as I'm leaving the room. His almost pleading, mine embarrassed.

* * *

I start to look forward to my time in Mrs. Johnson's office. Mostly, she wants me to stock the supply closet where they keep all the paper and clips and extra textbooks. Or I run the mimeograph machine, turning the crank until my wrist aches, then tucking flyers with their smudged purple print into the teacher cubbies. The work makes me feel chosen in a way I can't be in those teeming corridors. I can swish around the front desk and hand piles to the secretaries, who greet me with a "Hey, sweetie" or "Thanks, doll." The secretaries are always overwhelmed: phones ringing, some problem down on the second floor, security with their fizzing walkie-talkies rushing to break up a fight. Seems like every time I go in there, a couple of sullen and abashed kids are lined up on the bench, waiting. Or Mr. Stotter, who also looks overwhelmed, is in meetings with someone who's complaining. Twice I've seen Mrs. Rowan stepping into his office.

Once, I'm putting together some packets for the school elections when a boy shuffles out. I know him from art class—a small kid named Fred with a friendly smile. Today, though, he's glum. His mother follows, scowling, and then she raps his head, twice. I can see the back of his neck blush.

When I edge into the office, Mrs. Johnson is standing

by her desk, leaning ever so lightly on her fingertips. She seems to be swaying, like a great oak after a large wind has just passed through. She looks old—older than she's ever seemed before. For the first time, I notice a photograph of her with a man I figure is her husband. They're in bright summer clothes and sipping drinks with umbrellas. Seems so far away from here.

"I finished the packets," I whisper.

She doesn't move, but stays very still.

"The ones for the school elections. The rules and stuff?"

She nods, still without saying a word, a shiny welling-up in her eyes. "All my life I've fought against the names people call us." She still has her chin tucked, rubbing her lids. "And then I have a boy do this. Throw a chair across a room." She shakes her head. "Are we just living up to how they see us?"

It's like a needle that's pierced right through me, threaded with sadness. At this moment, she reminds me of my dad.

"Anything else you want me to do, Mrs. Johnson?"

"No, dear."

She motions toward the papers I set on her desk. "Thank you for this."

I pick up my bag and go to class. This is one of those times when I'm glad an adult told me what she thought.

CHAPTER 16

COLOR THEORY

The other big change in school is that the Community Circle class is finished. On our last day, Miss Griffith makes us all sit cross-legged in a circle, hold hands, and be our "best-intentioned selves." Then she hugs each one of us. I can still smell her smoky perfume when I leave.

Now, instead, I have art. I love everything about this room: the smell of turpentine, the stiff-crusted brushes in paint-splotched jars drying on a sill, the vanilla smell of new paper unfurling off the big roll. The teacher is young: Miss James, serious and calm. "Art isn't about everyone being an artist," she explains. "It's about teaching us to look at things differently. With fresh eyes. That's why the first thing you're going to look at is yourselves. We're going to do self-portraits."

Me and Tanisha are put at the same table. We sit across

from each other, perched on stools, with sheets of paper in front of us. Each of us has a mirror that we prop up against a wooden block. Tanisha settles down. I watch her stub of charcoal move across the page, expert and sure. My portrait is smudged and murky and the ears look like they're flapping off the sides of my head. When she's done, I glance over, amazed. She got everything right: the sharp chin, the slanted cheekbones and tough, flashing eyes. And the pucker in her brow, as if she's always a little mad or worried.

"Wow," I say. "That's really good."

One corner of her mouth lifts, an almost-smile.

"Tanisha's an artist," the girl next to her comments. "She makes pictures of all the women in her mother's salon."

I want to say, *I can see that.* But I don't. I nod.

"I draw all the time," she says softly.

When the bell rings, we shuffle off our stools, roll up our self-portraits and tuck them into the cubbies. I say to Tanisha, "I'd like to see your other stuff."

She turns, gives me a full-on smile. "Yeah. Maybe."

"Do you paint too?"

She shrugs. "When I can. One time my uncle brought me a whole set he got from his job. I used it a lot until my little brother messed it up." She adds, "He's always doing stuff like that."

"I wish I had a younger brother. Mine's big and bossy."

"I guess I'm the one who bosses. Especially since I got to take care of him all the time."

Just then a pack of girls comes down the hall. "Why you talking to her?" one hollers.

I see something cross Tanisha's face. Then fear, like a shadow. "I'm not!" She laughs and joins them in the flow.

This time I get it. She has to walk away. I know it's a show for them. Not me.

*   *   *

The next week in art, Miss James sets out different-colored square tabs stuffed into old Chock Full o' Nuts coffee cans. Our self-portraits are gone. We look around, puzzled.

"Today we're moving on to color. How we see it."

She's dragged out a big board, and now takes a green tab and sets it against a lime-green square. "Take a good look at this." Then she sets another tab against a magenta background. "Is it the same color?" she asks, pointing to the two panels.

"No!" most of the class choruses.

"You sure?"

"No way!"

"Yes," Tanisha calls. "It's the same."

"Tanisha's right."

"Whoo-hoo," a boy named Gerald hollers. "You're always the teacher's pet!"

She wiggles a little on her stool, pleased.

"That can't be!" another girl exclaims. "It's completely different."

It was true: one tab of green, against the light green backdrop, shimmers dark as an evergreen forest; the other is a pale aquarium wash. Our eyes switch back and forth. It doesn't make sense—the colors seem to be playing a trick on us.

"This is color theory, invented by a man named Josef Albers. A color's quality is always in relation to another color. Color is really about perception. It isn't stable."

She demonstrates a few more times, showing bands of color against each other, and squares within squares, and even one color in the middle with four different-shaded corners. Then she tells us to make our own—first by placing the tabs inside large squares, and then playing around with different combinations. The only real instruction is to try to use the same color and experiment in as many ways we can imagine, always changing our view.

Both Tanisha and I immediately grab for the paper and are swiftly swapping tabs around in front of us. It really is a game. Colors shimmer, slip around. Soon we're laughing and exclaiming over the groupings. "That can't be!" Tanisha laughs when I show her two combos I did with navy blue. We're so busy trying out our little exercises, the bell startles us. Tanisha blinks a few times, then frowns. "Already?"

"Sorry," Miss James says. "Let's put everything away. We'll be making notebooks out of these next week."

We spill out of class, still chatting, our heads buzzing. Darren appears and starts to walk with us. "What are y'all doing for Halloween?"

"Me and Josie and Francesca are going to walk around the neighborhood."

He grins. "Maybe I'll come with you."

I shake my head.

"I'm serious."

Tanisha says, "I'm doing up everyone's makeup. My little brother's a tiger. Rhonda's a crazy dead woman."

"Wow," I say.

"Wow is right," she says with a smile, and then saunters around the corner.

CHAPTER 17

GOBLINS

This Halloween is not like the old days. Me and Francesca and Josie used to pull on our costumes and trawl the courtyards of Cedar Gardens, filling up our plastic jack-o'-lanterns until our wrists hurt. Then, gorging ourselves on Tootsie Rolls and candy corn, we'd sit in the doorway of one of our apartments, swilling our hands in the bowls and giving out candy. That's when the teenagers would show up, in black vampire capes or with blue witch hair sprouting under dented hats. Then they were off, laughing, to some secret place of teenage-coolness. The next morning, there were raw eggs splattered on the pavement, blobs of shaving cream on tree branches.

This year we're neither here nor there. We feel too old

for trick-or-treating. But we're not part of the teenage packs. After an hour of half-hearted trick-or-treating, we dump our stash at Francesca's.

"Oh god," Francesca groans, flopping on her bed. "I am so bored!"

"Let's watch TV," Josie says. Sometimes the three of us will curl up together in Francesca's parents' bed to watch *The Brady Bunch*.

"You must be kidding." She swerves up, hands on her hips. "I don't want to stay home."

Her costume this year is basically what she wears all the time: a ribbed turtleneck that's starting to show the mounds of her breasts, a short suede skirt, and shiny boots. It's as if she's aiming to be a version of her mother. The only difference is the sparkle around her lids and her eyeliner, drawn super dramatic, Cleopatra-style.

Me and Josie are a muddle, as though we can't decide if we are or aren't dressed up. I'm in black—leotard, corduroys, and an old cape of Karim's that sags around my shoulders. Josie wears a peasant blouse tucked into a long print skirt, her hair swept into a matching scarf.

"Where do you want to go?"

Francesca shrugs. "I don't know. Let's just go walk."

So we lock up the house—Mr. and Mrs. George are out—and set out the bowl on the stoop with a sign that reads TAKE ONE. I feel a little shiver run up my arms. We don't usually trick-or-treat outside our courtyards. But we troop down the unfamiliar blocks, house after house. Now and then, I see clumps of teenagers.

"Hey," a voice calls.

Josie stiffens beside me. Francesca seems to be leaning toward them. "Hey back."

Their outlines begin to fill in: a few boys, no costumes. One smokes, the ember on his cigarette glowing red. It's the boys from Patty's. The ones who called out to us before.

Under the streetlamps the boys don't look so scary. There's something plain and ordinary about them—they all wear jeans and navy blue sweatshirts, the hoods flipped over the back collar of their denim jackets, and construction boots—as if they're already tired workingmen. One of the boys has a puffy baby face, a rash of pimples on his cheeks.

The loudest boy, Patrick, introduces himself and the others—Ryan, Joe, Bobby. They all mumble their hellos. Just kids. Francesca gives our names too.

"We seen you around," Patrick continues. "You especially." His eyes light on Francesca. She does look glamorous in her glossy boots.

"Really?" She giggles.

"Yeah. You live over there?" He's nodding toward the Cedar Gardens apartments.

"They do. I'm in the house on the corner."

"Oh yeah. Your old man have that convertible?"

"Yes!"

The other guys exchange looks. "That's some car," one of them remarks, but the way they say it makes me feel wobbly. As if it's an insult that her father would own such a nice car.

We chat a little more—one of them works at Patty's on the weekends. They go to the Catholic school, which is why we don't know them. They share Almond Joys and Reese's, and Ryan offers me his denim jacket when he sees I'm shivering. I wear it draped around my shoulders. It smells like boy sweat.

They tell us about all the pranks they usually do—twisting the swings up in the playground, shaving cream battles. Once they even threw a brick through a garage window. I look at Josie. That's not a prank.

"You wanna come up on the roof?" Patrick asks, pointing toward the apartment house at the end of the block.

"What's up there?" Francesca has her hips leaned up against a car, ankles crossed, as if this happened all the time.

"Eggs." He laughs, pointing to a shopping bag at his feet. "Already got ours."

"How do you get inside?"

"Friend of ours took care of it."

In the dark, I can see the whites of their eyes shine. This is a neighborhood I've never been to. My parents shrink away from these streets, scold me to avoid them.

Once, Karim got beat up by a group of boys when he went to play on their handball courts and that was that. "No need looking for trouble," my father explained.

But here they are inviting us, as if it's nothing. As if we're already teenagers.

We all begin walking toward the apartment house. When I turn to Josie, I see she hasn't moved. "What's the matter?" I call out.

"I'm not going." In her long, old-fashioned skirt and scarf, she looks like a character from *Little House on the Prairie*.

"Come on, Josie!" Francesca is happy.

"I can't."

"She is such a baby," Francesca mutters.

My heart turns like a burning rod in my chest.

"You're coming, right?" Francesca asks me.

I want so badly to go with Francesca, to finally feel that we are moving to something new. Wasn't this what this year was supposed to be about? But when I see Josie, with her soft face, I worry. It might never be the same between us again. She might never forgive me for choosing these boys.

"Please," I whisper. "Just for a few minutes. She can't go by herself. It'll be fun."

"I can't."

She looks so stubborn. Can't she just bend a little?

"I'm going home."

"Aww, come on," Patrick calls.

"Josie!" I say.

Too late. She's already gone into the shadows.

* * *

We go down the block, and duck into an alley on the side of the apartment building. Sure enough, a brick props open the metal door. We all press inside, muffling our laughter as we scramble past a boiler room, through another door, and then up an unlit stairwell. Three steep flights, until the last is a ladder leading to a door in the ceiling. Patrick goes first, using his big shoulder to push open the hatch door.

On the roof, Queens becomes a twinkling blanket, gray-pink haze softening the edges of the houses. The avenues are melting strands, cars moving like lit beads. I can even see Manhattan in the distance, the swoop of bridges strung across the river. Everyone scatters and oohs and aahs. A wisp of sadness brushes through me; I wonder if I can see all the way to John's neighborhood.

"Where you girls go to school?"

"I'm at Aldrich," Francesca says.

"Where's that?"

"In the city."

"Ooh. Fancy." Patrick smirks. "Your old man must have money." Francesca giggles. Now he's looking at me. "You?"

"JHS 241."

"The school a few blocks away?"

I hesitate. "No, it's in South Jamaica."

"Whoa. That's where the black kids go—"

I flinch. It's as if we've just fallen back on an electric fence. Singed.

"Hey, don't say that, stupid," a boy says. "Her dad—"

And mine, I want to say. My chest aches. I want to get out of here.

"Don't listen to him, man," Bobby puts in. "He's not prejudiced."

"Seriously," Patrick insists. "Is that safe? No way my folks would let my sister down there."

This is what darkness does. It hides who we are so we hear things we never did before. I see Francesca shrug the talk off. How many other things has she shrugged off, at her school too, with Evan? Is this what it's going to be, more and more, now that we're stepping outside Cedar Gardens?

Patrick begins reaching into the shopping bag, pulling out eggs. We can see the goblin shapes floating down below—capes and shiny astronaut costumes, glow-in-the-dark jack-o'-lanterns that merrily bob. A few eggs arc down. The shapes break apart, shrieking.

"Your turn!"

We hesitate. Patrick moves behind Francesca and embraces her, coaxing an egg into her palm. "Come on, you can do it." She leans her head into his chest, lets him guide her elbow out and over the ledge. A crack and another splatter. Someone curses. The boys laugh. The eggs go flying, more and more, though by now the goblin shapes know to shift to the other side of the street.

I'm losing track. The boys are tossing and whooping it up. I can't tell who is who. And where is Francesca? My eyes swerve around. Did others come up through the half door? I hear girls' voices, gruff as the boys, and they're dressed in the same way—faded jeans, navy hoods, denim jackets. They talk about girls and boys I don't know.

I really want to leave. Shrugging off the jacket, I set it on the ledge and search the wavering dark for Francesca. I can just make out two figures in a corner. Francesca? Then she's turning and running toward me. I can see how scared she is. I grab her arm.

As we're shifting toward the door, I hear someone ask, "You get far?"

"You know how they are."

They.

I yank her away. Then all I can hear is the clatter of our footsteps down the metal rails.

* * *

Back at Francesca's, we sit in her darkened living room, just the two of us. I want to yell at her, but she looks terrible, like a tossed-around doll. Occasionally the doorbell sounds. Teenage voices, kids we no longer want to join.

When she stops shaking, we go upstairs. I find her mom's Avon bubble bath, she runs a bath and undresses, leaving her turtleneck and miniskirt and tights in a pile on the floor. She seems small and fragile in the bubbles. After, she puts on a flannel nightgown. Its frilly yoke makes her look young, as if it's last year again.

"Will you stay with me?" she whispers. She's already on her quilt, knees up, heels tucked under.

"Yes."

I call my parents and then lie down beside her, slide an arm around her. She's all bones and shivering tiredness.

I hold on, as if we're one.

CHAPTER 18

SOME KIND OF PLACE

The next day wind and rain are whipping the leaves. No outside recess. I'm still shaken and sad from last night. Josie had been quiet on the bus but I didn't press her. I wind up with Darren across from me at the table in the library. I'm trying to get ahead on my Spanish homework, but he keeps tapping my wrist with his eraser. "How was Halloween?"

I wince. "Okay. Josie went home early. We hung out and . . ." I stop.

"Will you do me a favor?" he whispers.

"I can try."

He inches his chair closer. "Tell me this: Why doesn't Josie want to go with me?"

"I told you already. She doesn't go with boys."

"Why?"

"She just doesn't." I add, "She goes to church." I feel a pang, remembering her in her long skirt last night, walking away from us.

He makes a sucking noise with his teeth, mashes up his paper into a ball. "She can just give me a chance."

"I bet she'd give you more of a chance if you didn't get into fights."

He sits up, outraged. "I don't start it!"

"Whatever."

"I don't." But he sags in his chair.

We sit there, as if we're old friends. I think about how hard it is for all of us. The other girls over on the other side. Lucy proclaiming things. And maybe Tanisha was right. We do think we're better than the kids who live in this neighborhood. Isn't that what the adults have always been telling us? But what about the time Tanisha's wrist lifted up from her paper, her portrait blooming into view? I could never do that.

I can't stop thinking about art class and what happened to the colors. It's a lot like me and Josie and Francesca. The way we're seen depends on where we are. In our own neighborhood, we're just the same trio that everyone knows, three tan and brown girls who melt into each other. But here at JHS 241, Josie goes over to Angela and those other girls on the handball courts. At her private school, Francesca is the fast halfie girl with real curves who gets kissed in a room.

And me?

On Halloween night I wanted to transform into someone older. Those boys' words singed. But I just hid in the dark and let their insults cover me. A hot shame sweeps through me. What am I? I just blend, depending on where I am. Playing it safe.

Then I notice Darren is eyeing my pile, noticing my novel. "What's that about?"

"It's called *The Pearl*."

"You read the whole book?"

"Of course!"

He shakes his head. "What's it about?"

When I start to explain the story, he gets really intense. I see a kind of hunger in his eyes. I realize: What I think of as being pushy is just that Darren wants to know, a lot. He's hungry. Not just for pizza and fries. For other stuff too. To find out what's in my book. Why Josie won't go out with him.

"Here," I say, and push it toward him. "Take mine."

At first he makes a face, as if the book smells. But then he fingers the cover and starts to leaf through the pages. His body goes still. He reads for the rest of the period.

* * *

After school I'm surprised to find Josie waiting for me on the front steps. That doesn't happen too much these days. "Sorry about leaving last night," she says.

"It's okay. You did the right thing."

"You want to come home with me?"

Joy surges through me. "Yes!"

Just like the old days: Mrs. Rivera greeting me, as if I'm a long-lost relative. "Josie, where've you been hiding your friend?" she asks. I savor that word, *friend.* "Remember when you used to dance and do your boots song?"

"Mom," Josie groans now. "You're embarrassing her!"

Mrs. Rivera gives a little tug on one of Josie's pigtails. "I embarrass you all the time these days, don't I?"

Suddenly, I miss everything about Josie: her mom, teasing us, standing in the kitchen in her housedress, her close-cropped hair. Her soft Jamaican accent that somehow chides too. I miss Josie's room: the picture of her and her brother, Manuel, on a beach in Puerto Rico when they went to visit her dad's family; and her huge dollhouse, built by Mr. Rivera in his spare time. Saturdays we'd snip fabric scraps for the curtains or use Mrs. Rivera's batter and make tiny pancakes for the doll family's breakfast. And then swallow them down laughing.

We slide down to the floor and begin rearranging the miniature rooms, whispering vignettes with her family of dolls. It's like touching a soft part in me I forgot. A groove between us, old and familiar. Though we could never talk about that on the bus or in school. We put on a few records—first *The Partridge Family,* a show we sometimes watch together. Then *Sly and the Family Stone,* which Josie borrowed from her brother and makes us feel older.

As we're singing along, her mother calls up to us,

"Time to start on homework. Jamila, you're more than welcome to work here."

The table is inviting: a waxy cloth with bright fruit designs, two slabs of fresh cake, the molasses taste melting in our mouths. A pitcher of punch tinkles with ice.

To my surprise, Mrs. Rivera sets out two math textbooks: Josie's, which is green, and a red one like mine, from the SP program. "Every night Josie does double homework. We're having Josie keep up with what you do," Mrs. Rivera says. She adds, "We can thank you for that."

"Me?" My voice is a squeak.

"Josie mentioned how you noticed the difference in your textbooks."

I look at her. "You told me you didn't care about that!"

Josie blushes. "I know. But you were right." She wrinkles her nose and bites into her cake. "I am so sick of math!"

"Too bad," Mrs. Rivera says, but she's smiling.

I'm flooded with happiness, and amazed at the doubled-up textbooks: It reminds me of how Mr. Rivera got into Cedar Gardens, calling and showing up at the rental office, persisting until they gave in. Now I can see why Josie has such a quiet, dogged strength. Strong isn't about mouthing off. Or picking a fight. It's about knowing how to make a space for herself, in her own way.

* * *

That night after dinner, I drag the phone into my room and call John. "What's up?" He's happy to hear from me.

139

Especially since I work for Mrs. Johnson three lunchtimes a week and we don't see each other as much.

I take a breath. But today it hit me. All that piping up in Mrs. Markowitz's class isn't really me. The tough girl. I'm not supposed to copy Karim. He makes me anxious, as if it's my job to keep up. Part of me doesn't want to do that. I like slowing things down. Being with Josie and still playing dolls or talking with John on the phone and not kissing. I want to go back and forth. I don't want to wind up like Francesca, frightened and curled up in a flannel nightgown. I want to be big in a different way, my own way.

"I know how to get Josie into SP," I say.

He laughs. "Miss Fix-It."

"You bet." And I laugh too.

* * *

"Mrs. Johnson?"

"Yes?"

I'm standing in her office, with a stack of flyers warm with new ink. I step closer to her desk. "My friend Josie. She was always in the gifted classes with us. She just—she didn't do too good on the test."

"*Well* on the test," she corrects me.

I flush. All the words are jamming up in my head. "Yeah. But she's really smart. It's just she needs to take her time with things. And there's my friend Darren, he's—"

"Slow down, slow down," she says with a laugh. Today

140

her outfit is all green: crinkly green jacket, pleated pale green skirt, and olive flats so she isn't so scarily tall. "I know Darren. Too well, I'm afraid."

"He's really smart too."

"Smart-mouthed, you mean?" Though her voice is stern, I can see her eyebrows lift with mischief.

"Can I show you something?"

It feels funny, leading a grown-up. But something has come over me, a quiet, steady part of me I got from Josie. I take her down the corridor to the supply room, which she has to unlock with her jangling keys. "See how they get this one?" I ask, running a finger down the spine of a biology textbook. "And we get another?"

She nods.

"How will they ever catch up?"

"Maybe they won't."

"That isn't fair!"

"No," she says. "A lot of things aren't fair."

I set my hands on my hips. "I think they need another chance."

"The testing is out of our hands, Jamila. It's citywide."

"But we took it so long ago! What if they've changed? Or what if it was a bad day? What if someone was hungry?"

"True—"

"Like with Darren. He lives in some attic somewhere; I bet he doesn't have any place to study. Maybe you could make some kind of place."

Mrs. Johnson goes still.

"Kids could study together. Kind of buddy up."

"I like that! I can put out a sign, Study Club!"

"No signs. That's kind of embarrassing. Nothing . . ." I hesitate.

"Go ahead. Speak your mind."

"Dumb. Or too . . . corny. Everyone will make fun of it and won't go."

She laughs. "Okay. Point taken."

"Just some quiet place. You could even make it a kind of secret. You have to be invited. And they could work together. Help each other. So . . ." I pause. "They can see each other different. See themselves different."

"See themselves *differently*." Mrs. Johnson's head angles to the side. She looks at me a long time, until my forehead starts to sweat. Maybe she's going to scold me, or tell me again that I'm over the line. But then I see her tight smile.

"You may be a toughie with fire, Jamila," she murmurs. "But you've got heart."

CHAPTER 19

WINGMAN

All through the rest of November and into December, I watch Josie and Darren work together, side by side. We use a little room in the library with a big round table that takes up most of the space. Mrs. Johnson warns "No funny stuff" from Darren—meaning no joshing around, no distractions. I think he was so shocked and grateful that he was allowed to be in a room with Josie for a solid fifty-two minutes that he would have laid down on the carpet and recited fractions the entire time. Every few nights I give the report about Josie and Darren over the phone to Francesca, how they're getting along and how Josie's pushed far ahead in math. "I knew you'd figure something out!" she says.

The day before Christmas break, me and John swap presents. We're standing at the entrance of school, kids teeming around us. We tear open the wrapping, our boxes the exact same size. I draw mine out of the square of fluffy cotton: a silver bracelet with two snakeheads just barely touching. I've seen a lot of the South Jamaica girls wear them, heavy silver clinking maturely on their arms. I slip mine on, feel its cool, heavy weight. Something strong and serious lies between us. Even though we've kissed only once.

John takes his out—a plated bracelet too, the chained kind boys can wear—with a big "J," for either John or Jamila. His grin is wide, and he latches his over his cuff and lets it jiggle. We're suddenly shy with each other.

"Hey, you two love birds, bus is going!" Darren calls.

I can't stop grinning and looking at my bracelet.

*   *   *

That week, slushy rain freezes the puddles into stiff peaks. We sleep late most mornings and Dad wakes us up whistling as he cooks fried eggs and toast. I keep twirling my bracelet, waiting for someone to say anything. But they don't even notice. Mom lets me go shopping once the sales start since I've grown two inches and my new corduroy bell-bottoms are too short. I keep fantasizing that I'll step on an escalator and John will come coasting down the other side, smiling.

For two days we visit Mom's college roommate, Ellie Roesner, in Connecticut. She and her family live in a house that's so old, it's got one of those split Dutch doors. I hang out with their young daughter, Pammie, up in the attic while Daddy and Mr. Roesner go into the basement, where they build a chair. I haven't seen him that relaxed in a long time.

We come back in time for New Year's, which we spend at Josie's place. Francesca's parents have some business party in the city, but Francesca is with us, quieter than usual. Mr. Rivera has brought packets of sweets from Puerto Rico, and we tilt cardboard hats on our heads. At one point he flings open the patio doors and shows us how to dance until Mrs. Rivera calls out, "Come back here right now! This isn't San Juan!" But Mr. Rivera swings out an arm and pulls Mrs. Rivera tight, the two of them swaying. Francesca watches closely, wiping the wetness from her eyes.

* * *

The first day back from break, Mrs. Johnson waves me into her office and makes me shut the door. She looks almost giddy. "I have some news."

"What?"

"There's a new program for students who have been identified as on the cusp academically. They can take a test at the end of the school year, and if they do well, they can enter the summer program."

"And?"

"And then at the end of that, the board of ed will see about their placement."

Sounds like a lot more door flaps to crawl through.

But it's something. And I know Josie can do it. I hope Darren can too.

All through February and March the two of them keep at it. One day the principal pops his head in and gives us the thumbs-up, declares the two of them are showing "perseverance." When the door shuts, Darren leans back in his chair and comments, "You hear that? We have per-se-*veeer*-ence."

Josie giggles.

"Not per-se-*cuuu*-tion."

"Vocabulary word!" Josie chimes. "You get that one?"

"Last week." He picks up his spiral notebook, which is all bent and creased, covered in ink scribbles. "My sentence was: Miss Daly, my math teacher, has a persecution complex."

"How?" Josie asks.

"She takes it personally when we don't do our homework."

"That means she cares," Josie replies.

"I get that. Why you always so serious all the time?"

"Hush," I tell them sternly. "You're not supposed to be talking!"

"Yes, Miss Bossy," he says with a grin.

And most of the time they really do the work, since they've promised each other they are going to do the summer program. Darren has a way of glancing at Josie, mischief flashing in his face, and I can see her blush, smile to herself. She's not as guarded. Darren is almost an extra brother—better than Karim, who is usually in a grouchy teenage mood, acting like any contact with his kid sister is as bad as catching the plague.

On another day—maybe because I got through a whole class with Mrs. Markowitz without a problem—after dance class I find myself tugging on my jeans next to Johanna, ready to talk to her. Of course in dance, Johanna is the best. For the concert she's the one who stands at the top of our V formation, her long arms guiding us in our complicated number to the *Mission Impossible* theme song.

"So you know there's this study club I created—"

She raises her eyebrows, skeptical. "You?"

"Yeah. With Mrs. Johnson—"

"And?" She's already hiked her bag over her shoulder.

"I thought maybe the student council could create a couple more like that. Keep them small. People have buddies to work with."

Surprise passes over her face. "You should be my campaign manager."

I notice she doesn't ask. "What does that mean?"

"Put up posters. Give out flyers. Get the word out."

Be your lackey, I want to snap back. But then I realize: maybe it's not such a bad idea. Johanna is popular in a good way. Kids actually listen to her, half the time because they're in love with her, and half the time because they're afraid. And maybe I can learn something from her too.

"Think about it," she says.

And then she floats off, shoulders back, head tipped

high. I wonder if she'll take all the credit for what I created. I don't mind. All I care is that I've done something good. And that I've begun to belong.

*   *   *

Evening and another out of the ordinary experience: Me and Karim are actually sitting in the living room alone with each other. Our parents have decided to go out to the movies like teenagers on a date, Daddy guiding Mom into the car with his hand at her back. Watching them, I feel happy in a way I haven't since I got in trouble at school. My parents are A-OK sometimes.

"What's up, kiddo?" Karim murmurs as I drop down on the sofa next to him. His eyes stay on the TV, watching the news, while he runs a copper brush on his suede boots. I'm happy that he used his old nickname for me.

"Nothing much."

"You liking your new school?"

"It's better than before."

He gives the boot a vigorous swipe before taking up the other boot. Walter Cronkite is giving the same old reports on Vietnam. It's bad.

"How so?"

I pause because I'm not sure I know what I want to say. Karim always has to throw down a challenge. When he glances at me I feel his dare.

"So I did this cool thing," I begin.

"Uh-huh."

"In my school, there are a lot of kids that get in trouble. And my friend Darren, he's one of those . . ."

His brush is making hard strokes; his eyes are on the TV. How can I make him see the importance of what I've done? And then I explain about the study club, and the bonus of Josie being willing to hang out with Darren, how he's had such a crush on her and, before, she wouldn't give him the time of day. I keep waiting for Karim to glaze over, or elbow me out with impatience. But I don't stop talking. About how the school is really tough but now I'm going to be Johanna's campaign manager. As I speak, I realize there are other ways to feel big.

When I'm done, he sets his brush down and says, "So you're a wingman?"

"What's that mean?"

"The side guy, who helps out the main guy."

"I guess."

Is that a bit of admiration shining in his eyes? "Not bad, kiddo. What made you want to do that?"

"I don't know. I was so mad about Josie and I thought Johanna should know about it."

"You still mad?"

I pause. "I guess. But more about John. Not getting to hang out."

"You should talk to Dad about your cowboy. Maybe he'll let you see him."

I look at him in horror. "He'd never agree!"

He shrugs. "You never know. Especially if you don't

try." I wish I could talk to Karim more. Only he knows what it's like, this weird mix we are, where we don't know what people make of us. We've grown up with our parents' stories of daring to get married. But what about us? At school they're always talking about how we're a great experiment, a new age. But they didn't tell us about this. How we keep banging into a lot of the past.

And maybe this is what growing up means. I'll be thirteen in a few months. Maybe it isn't a Ferris wheel swooping down and going one way. It's a back and forth. Some days you're curled in eleven, playing with your best friend's dollhouse, and other days you're putting gloss on your lips and ignoring some boys staring at you.

He stands, stretches his arms. "How long I have to babysit you, anyway?"

* * *

"Daddy?"

"Yes?" My father looks up from the tiny desk crammed in a corner of their bedroom. His blueprints are rolled out on the bed.

I suck in my breath. "Can John and his friend come hang out?"

He sets down his glasses. Without them, he looks vulnerable, his eyes liquid and black.

"What's your idea?"

Daddy is always very still. What I want to say is that when I look at John, the same wave of quiet comes over me. When Daddy talks, everyone listens because he carefully lays out his words, as if he's building something. His way of speaking comes from a lot of considering. I wish I could explain how John is not so different. I feel hushed and good when he talks to me.

But I've lost all the bravery from yesterday with Karim.

"Go on." Daddy's voice is soft.

"Maybe they could take the bus and come visit."

"When?"

I twist in my shoes. "The weekend?"

He nods. "With who?"

I panic. I hadn't thought that far in advance. But my father is leading me. "With me and Josie. And maybe Francesca."

"Does she know them?"

"No. But I don't think she's got a whole lot of friends at her school."

"I imagine that's so." He pauses. "Still, I'd prefer if you had an activity. Just hanging around doesn't sound promising."

We could maybe bring them to Patty's for our comic book and fried eggs ritual. Then I remember those boys on the roof, their ugly words.

The other day I was getting off the bus and I saw posters for the spring fair tacked on telephone poles. Every year there's an amusement park outside in the church parking lot; in the basement they sell trinkets and homemade gifts, candied popcorn, and baked treats.

"There's the spring fair. We could go to that."

"Not a bad idea."

"It'll be great! I can get a gift for Mother's Day and—"
I want to say something more about John, but I stop.

He rubs the fold over his nose, slips his glasses back on.
He's back to being his usual self—no-nonsense. "That's all
you're going to do, yes?"

"I promise."

"All right, then." His blueprint paper rustles as he turns
around in his swivel chair. "But you make sure those boys
introduce themselves first."

CHAPTER 20

SILVER

We can see the Ferris wheel turning from a few blocks away, and the octopus ride waving its silver blinking arms. The tinny music threads toward us.

Francesca and Josie and I had waited at the bus stop for John and Darren, hands jammed into our new spring jackets, nervously stamping our boots. Francesca complained, "I'll be a fifth wheel!" "Oh, stop being so dramatic," we told her. "It'll be fun with you." She was grateful, I think. Someone had scrawled *Francesca = Slut* on the bathroom door at her school, which made her stuff her face into a pillow and cry all last weekend.

We had stopped at home. Darren was shyer than usual, and I couldn't help noticing the dirty fur on his parka hood and too-short sleeves. A smiling Daddy shook their hands, interviewed them briefly, offered us sodas, and then sent us on our way, with a firm deadline of five o'clock so the boys could be home by a safe hour.

"Your old man's all right." Darren laughed as we left my apartment.

"He's strict," John says. "Like my nana."

"Yeah, but your nana know how to cook. I listen to anyone who cooks like that." Darren punches John's arm. I knew from John how often Darren was over at his house, scarfing down Nana's roast chicken and beans.

We dawdle in the courtyards, getting to know each other in a new way. Darren gives John a shove so he goes crashing into a hedge, the last of the frost shaking loose. Josie and Darren walk together, about a foot between them, Darren making goofball jokes. But it's easy, since they're used to each other now.

Then we stop in our old playground and take turns on the swings, even though the cold chains bite our palms. I feel like a visitor to my own childhood, remembering me and Josie and Francesca pushing our knees into the air for hours until our mothers' voices urged us home in the dwindling light. But with boys, this place has a new sparkle. It's everything I want—to feel normal with them on my own streets.

We head to the fair, which is spread out in the big parking lot next to the church. A banner flutters over the entrance: WELCOME TO THE SPRING FAIR!

After we waste five dollars in a shooting gallery, we start to wander the noisy stalls. We run into Manuel and

Karim, who say hello to the boys. As we move away, my brother pulls me aside, and says quietly, "Watch yourself here." I nod, and shake him off. Karim can be so annoying.

Francesca points to the Ferris wheel, which casts its silver mass against a bright blue sky. "We have to do that!" she cries.

"Not me," Darren says. "That stuff makes me sick."

"Me too," John adds.

So the three of us climb onto a swaying seat, feel the hard metal bar clang down across our laps. Terrified, I shut my eyes. But I am wedged between Josie and Francesca, our thighs pressed tight together. We're shaking and breathing as one.

"Ready?" Francesca asks.

"Yes!" Josie says.

"Come on, Jamila, you have to look!"

And I do. Because it's the three of us, dangling at that perfect spot at the top. And then the plunge down. Over and over, the wheel sweeps up and around.

*   *   *

When we return to the ground, the boys are waiting but their faces seem a little clouded.

"You okay?" I ask John.

"Yeah, fine," he mumbles.

But something shut down in him. We get some cotton candy and walk, scooping it into our mouths.

Why hadn't I noticed it before? We might blend but

155

John and Darren stick out. My mother never goes anywhere without doing a scan of a room on my father's behalf. I set my hand on John's wrist, feel the bracelet I gave him in December, cool and solid.

Then I spy a little striped tabby stuffed animal at the Ball and Basket game—small basketball hoops. "Get me that?" I ask sweetly, taking John's arm.

"I don't have much of a shot."

Francesca chimes in, "You can do it!"

Just as she gives him a teasing nudge, I have a weird sensation. As if someone is tracking the backs of my legs. I swivel my head and get bumped by a bunch of kids streaming past. Then I see them next to a ticket booth. Those boys. The ones from the roof.

One of them grins and calls out, "Go on! Bet you got a killer dunk!"

I don't like the way they say that. I'm not sure the others heard.

"Let's go inside." I try to keep the strain out of my voice.

"I want to see John shoot!" Darren says. "And what about that cat?"

"It's okay. I don't want it."

Darren shrugs. "Whatever."

We pause on the stairs leading down to the church basement. I can hear a crush of voices below. Downstairs there's so much stuff, my eyes hurt: baskets of sugar cookies, stands of beaded necklaces, a vintage table with beaded purses and lace doilies, another of cigar boxes pasted with pictures.

We're hungry, so we head to the food booths, buying a bag of fried dough balls dusted in confectioner's sugar. Then we stroll the aisles, the powder making rings around our mouths. More tables: candlesticks, felt cushions, pale pink and blue blankets, and baby socks. Crocheted vests in rainbow colors. "These I have to have!" Francesca exclaims.

"We're not here to shop for us," Josie reminds her.

"Just a sec."

I can't help but see in Francesca what's always been there: She's hungry—for things, and more things. She can't wait for anything—growing up too. It makes me sad, wishing Francesca would just slow down.

"Come on, y'all. This is boring," Darren complains.

"One more!" She twirls. "What do you think?"

"How much that granny thing cost?" He goes to touch the dangling label.

And then I see them again: the boys. They've followed us and are watching us from a few tables away.

"Let's go," I whisper to John.

"Where?"

"Out."

"Why?"

"It's late."

"But we just got here!"

There's no logic to my feelings. Under those eyes, I

tighten my hold on John's jacket sleeve, feel the muscle beneath.

Francesca loops her hands through Darren's and Josie's arms, passes right by those boys, oblivious as Patrick's eyes follow her. She stops at some multicolored scarves. Bored, Darren shifts to a nearby table displaying antique silver, turning over the spoons, idly running his finger on the patterns.

A woman leans over. "Put that back!"

He looks up. "What'd you say?"

"I said put it back."

"I didn't take nothin'," he mutters.

The woman wriggles out from behind the table. She's wearing a big sweater with a triangle pattern across the chest. "Let's see."

"I told you. I didn't take nothin'." Darren rolls back on his heels, elbows drawn in tight to his body. I've seen that in him before—in the halls or with Mrs. Johnson— readying for a fight.

In the background the boys advance, as if one person, with Patrick in the lead. I feel that heat pulsing. *Don't you remember us?* I want to ask. Of course they do. Francesca especially.

Patrick's eyes. The set of his mouth. They want to smash this picture. "You better leave."

It hits me that the woman in the sweater is related to him. She calls out, "Patrick, let it go."

"You gotta leave," he repeats.

"No I don't."

"Now." His legs are in a wide stance.

"Patrick, that's enough now—"

"I got this, Aunt Jean."

Don't, don't, I think, watching Darren, the anger that's ticking inside him. He kicks a leg. The table caves in, silverware sliding off the top, knives and forks and teaspoons twirling with a clatter to the floor.

"That's it!"

Patrick goes flying toward him and starts pushing him hard. The other boys follow.

"Stop!" the woman cries.

I turn to her, furious. "Then you shouldn't have started it!"

John unlatches from me and joins in too, which only makes it worse. Patrick and his friends pull them both down the aisle, through the back door, and out into the parking lot, where the boys—three, four, five of them— swing and kick at John and Darren. Francesca is weeping. Josie is so stunned she can't move. I go blank with fear, and even though I hear myself shouting to stop, it's as if no one hears.

"Hey!"

"Hey, cut that out!"

I swerve to see Karim running toward me. Manuel is right behind, leather jacket flying. They tackle the boys hard, wrench Patrick away by the shoulders. A few more fists fly but the other boys start to stagger away. Manuel and Karim are older by a couple of years.

When the boys finally leave, hiking their jeans and wiping their mouths, there is John, crumpled against the wall. He has a bloody nick on one side of his mouth and his jacket is pulled off his shoulder. Karim reaches over to straighten him up. I see something I've never seen before in Karim: The fights he was in all these years. His own scar over his eye.

Darren lies on the ground, not even moving. And then I notice the nub of his ankle bone, bare skin. He has no socks.

CHAPTER 21

FATHERS

I don't think I ever was so glad to see my father.

He takes one look at John and Darren and knows exactly what happened. His face goes ashen and drawn, older. He takes them upstairs and blots their cuts with disinfectant and puts on Band-Aids. Francesca sits sobbing on a chair. "I hate them. I hate living here," she keeps saying.

The boys trudge downstairs, freshly washed, and sit in the living room, hushed. "Yes, sir" and "no, sir" is all they manage to say. My dad has given Darren a pair of socks that droop off his feet. John keeps biting his lip, staring at the floor. It gives me a sharp pain, seeing the Band-Aid slanted across one cheek. I feel dirty, a girl who lives in a neighborhood that does this.

"You all right?" my dad asks Karim, who has remained, hovering.

He nods. "Yes, sir." It's the first time Karim has called Daddy that in a long time.

Daddy adds, "I remember that time I had to pull some boys off you too."

A scowl flickers across Karim's face and then his gaze goes a little hurt.

"You did a good thing, son. Manuel did too."

Then my father turns back to Darren and John and asks a lot of questions. Standing, he says, "My wife, Penny, will talk to the girls later. Maybe we can track down the boys. Speak to the church."

"Leave it alone," Darren mumbles.

"We can't," Josie says.

Josie crosses the room, puts her arm around Darren. He's breathing, fast. His fists are clenched on his knees. She doesn't say anything. She just keeps her arm on his shoulders, and his breathing slows.

* * *

We drive John and Darren back in the same pained silence. My father had fed everyone grilled cheese sandwiches and then sent Francesca and Josie home.

I sit quiet beside my father, the two boys in the back.

It's all my fault.

We turn down one narrow street after another until we arrive at Darren's, the gloomiest one, with so many busted streetlights. He tells us to stop in front of a worn house, its porch sprouting old junk, a refrigerator. Only one dim light shines in a window, behind a sheet tacked to the panes.

"You want me to speak to your mother?" my father asks.

"Nah, she's not home."

"Anyone home?"

"It's okay."

Before we can say anything, he's angled out of the car and slipped down the narrow alley.

*   *   *

At John's house the two fathers match each other in some way: my father leaning forward, rail-thin, hands pressed on the table. Mr. Wayne, broad-faced, with tufts of gray-ish hair at his temples. His voice rumbles, low and gravely, with a Southern drawl. He also wears cardigans with leather buttons.

"We are so very sorry," my father repeats. "If we had known—"

"Can't never know in cases like that."

"Yes, but your son was our guest. We should have pro-tected him."

John's father shakes his head and sets his hand on

John's waist. "Son, you go and rest. Don't need to be listening to this."

"But, Dad—"

"Go on."

I ache for John to look at me one more time before he leaves. But he keeps his eyes lowered, whispering, "Yes, sir," and is gone.

Nana shuffles into the room. "We tell them all the time to be careful going to other neighborhoods. 'Specially these days."

My head hangs. So it *is* our fault. Living in a place that doesn't want them. Or us.

"You teach your children to mind themselves," Mr. Wayne comments. "To turn a cheek. I say this to the young ones who preach all that radical talk and fighting back."

My father agrees. "I say that to my son too."

Mr. Wayne shakes his head. "I don't like to say this. But sometimes turning away isn't enough."

"No." My father sighs. "Sometimes it isn't."

* * *

That night, I hear my parents talking softly at the table. I creep down the stairs and sit leaned up against the banister, listening.

"That boy," he murmurs.

"John?"

"No, the other one."

"Darren."

"I had a friend like that. Melvin. Melvin lived in everyone's houses. Everyone knew his mother was crazy. We took care of him."

I go motionless. My father almost never talks about his childhood in Barbados. Everything with him is moving forward, here, now—whatever can be organized, planned, traced out with a mechanical pencil.

"Where is he now?" my mother asks.

"He didn't wind up anywhere good." My father sounds wistful. "You know, someone like me shows up at a construction site. You think those guys like it when I tell them all they did wrong? Those boys at the church. That's their fathers." He shakes his head. "Why do we let our children into this? It's one thing if I choose—"

She sets her hand on his. "What else can we do?"

"Maybe we should move to the suburbs. Not Long Island. Maybe Connecticut, like Ellie. You know I wouldn't mind a little workshop to tinker in."

"You want to live in a place where you have to explain yourself all the time?"

"We do that now. We can be firsts."

"I'm tired of being first."

"But the schools—"

"I know."

They go quiet. I see Mom's pale, heart-shaped face under the lamp, her thin fingers twined in his. I love them so much right then.

* * *

It's a glum Monday. The gray outside presses through our windows like washed-out rags.

After third period, turning a corner, I spot John. I feel shaky. Maybe he isn't mad. Maybe from now on, I can stay just an hour in his neighborhood and my father will pick me up. Or we can spend time on Jamaica Avenue strolling past the stores. I want to squeeze my arms around his neck, whisper all this in his ear. Be brave together. He stops several inches away, guarded.

Chilled metal is pressed into my palm. "Sorry," he says.

This time I know to keep my mouth shut. I look down. The "J" of his bracelet glimmers up at me.

There's hot grit in my eyes and I can't stop blinking. "What—why?"

I see the tears swimming up in his gaze. I love John's eyes.

"It's too hard." He's searching and he swallows.

"But we can talk! And I can come see you and—"

"Stop."

I burst out, "You're a coward, John Wayne! Nothing like the cowboy!"

He shakes his head, takes a step away. He's surprised by the bite in my voice.

"No. I—I just can't go over your place, that's all."

I feel awful. He's the one who can't blend. Who got

beat up. A Band-Aid across his cheek. "I know! I'm sorry. I didn't mean that—" I try not to cry.

He's taken a few more steps back. "You can keep yours."

Then he's gone, into the swell of kids. Something folds shut in me.

CHAPTER 22

CHANGE

I don't want to do anything. Not work for Mrs. Johnson, not help Johanna with the election. I write John notes over and over again and crumple them up. *I am so sorry. I've got a temper. You are brave. You are strong.* I stare at the phone. I lie in bed at night, close my eyes and imagine it's fall again and we're in the schoolyard and he's sliding that bandana from my neck as the sky blazes yellow with leaves. Or I'm watching how his lashes sweep down when we squeeze in a few words on the front school steps. I don't want time to stand still at the top of that Ferris wheel. I want to circle back.

On Saturday, Josie and I have a sleepover at Francesca's and they try to make me feel better. We paint each other's toenails and do our Cheez Doodles and cream cheese routine. "Oh my god." Francesca sighs. "It's our first breakup!"

"My first breakup," I remind her.

"Do you miss kissing him?"

"I only kissed him once." It isn't the kissing I miss. It's the being together. The phone calls.

The next Monday and Wednesday, Darren doesn't show for study club. At first we think he's sick, but then Josie and I see him at lunch, hanging on the benches with some girls. They give us the cut-eye look, but they don't come over. My heart seizes up. Josie says nothing. We do our study club, just the two of us, but it's not the same. That happens twice more. Josie spends the time working her way through some stapled sheets Mrs. Johnson gave her for applying to the summer program.

"What is wrong with you?" Johanna asks me one day outside school when she notices I haven't handed out any of the flyers she'd given me. I don't know how she does it, but Johanna looks even taller than before. "You were supposed to put them up at lunch."

"Sorry."

She peers a little closer. "Are you sick or something?"

I try to move toward the lineup of buses. "Can we just not talk about it?"

"Are you my campaign manager or what?" she calls after me.

I whirl around. "I don't know!"

On the bus I sit next to Josie, my books gathered on my lap, mouth shut. The sand-colored school shrinks and flattens as we pull away.

*   *   *

"Enough."

Josie presses her palms on the table and stands. The cafeteria roars as everyone chucks their trays and heads outside. We have our free period and are supposed to go to study club next.

Josie swerves down the aisles of tables and outside. I follow as she marches up to Darren and the girls.

Darren's got his legs stretched out, one arm draped on the back of the bench. "Whassup, Josie?"

"You can't," she says.

"Can't what?"

"Give up."

A couple of girls giggle. I'm so nervous I stay a little behind. I'm not used to Josie like this. Definitely not in front of other kids.

"Aw, come on. It's not such a big deal."

"It is. We've got a test to take."

"Summer school's stupid."

"And you're smart."

He lets out a slow smile. "You want to spend it in some hot old classroom?"

Her eyebrows knot. "You made a promise."

"Yeah I did. But what's it matter? Y'all know what they

170

think of me anyway." He turns a little, facing one of the girls.

Josie steps closer. Her hands in fists on her hips. "You get yourself to our study club now, you hear?"

"Oooh, Darren. Looks like your girl is bossing you."

"She's not his girl," I pipe in.

"Sure sounds like it."

Josie blushes, hard. But she doesn't move.

Slowly, his long legs unfolding, Darren stands. "All right," he mumbles. "Don't have to make such a fuss."

* * *

There's a different light in Francesca's house. None of the lamps are turned on. The sheer curtains are shut across the patio doors. Francesca is sitting on the velvet couch, feet tucked beneath her.

"What's going on?" I ask. She called us both up the minute we got home. Usually she comes home from school much later.

"I didn't go to school today."

"You sick?"

She shakes her head. "No." She pats the sofa. Josie and I sit on either side.

"So I'm not going back to Aldrich."

"That's good!" I say. "We can be together!"

"I guess."

I'm already thinking. Next year: eighth grade. Josie in SP, Francesca too. It has to be better.

"It's because . . ." She turns her head away.

"Francesca?" Josie asks.

"My mom and dad. They're separating." She looks at us, stricken.

That can't be. Our moms and dads can't split up. It's always been three families, the firsts. Sitting on the patio here, the dads joking. Mr. George with a beautiful vase he wants to show them, Mrs. George's legs crossed, her cigarette smoke twisting into the air. Sure, the Georges fought a lot. But not this.

"I guess my mom's mad at him. Says he spends money like there's no tomorrow." She sighs. "They may even sell the house." Her voice is small.

"They can't!"

"Anyway, there's no money for private school. My mom says we have to change how things are done."

"Wow," we both say, and hug her.

We sit on the couch, holding hands. Quiet. I don't know what else to say. This year, twelve to thirteen, has so much hard change.

This change hurts the most.

CHAPTER 23

TECTONICS

"Get up, sleepyhead."

Daddy jiggles my ankle. I thrust my foot deeper into the warm quilt.

"Up and at 'em. We're taking a drive."

I groan. Usually that means some boring visit to somewhere in the city where we stare at an empty lot and he explains the building his company will put there.

I drag myself out of bed and dress. I have to admit, as we get into the car, it's a pretty day. Pink blossoms are blooming on the two craggy trees outside our courtyard. The ground is soft and fresh-smelling. To my surprise, this time Daddy drives across the George Washington Bridge, sun glancing off the spires, and then up a winding road on the Jersey side. The Palisades are to our right—great cliffs that drop to the Hudson River.

I've been here before with my father, and sure enough, he parks. Keys cupped in his palm, coat unbuttoned, he leads me to the bench by the lookout, and we sit there awhile, not speaking. Bushes and trees are dusted with light green. The Hudson slips past like a moving sheet of glass.

"You have a long face these days, Jamila. What's been happening with you?"

I push my fists into my jacket pockets. The last thing I want to do is tell my father anything about my life. Then I blurt, "John broke up with me."

He nods. "I see. That's too bad. He's a nice boy."

"We can't hang out. We can't do anything." I add, "He hates me after what happened."

"Oh, darling," he says. "He doesn't hate you. He's hurt."

I shake my head. "You don't know. I said . . . stupid things to him."

He leans back on the bench and considers this.

"You lose your temper?"

I nod.

"This whole business was hard on everyone. Those two good boys . . ." He pats my knee. "You see that cliff there?"

I look over at a rise of ground, north of us.

"Not far away from here is a place called Lamont Earth Observatory. Did you know I came all the way from Barbados to work for a professor who is part of that place?"

"No."

174

"This man and the men he worked with came up with something new for geology. They call it plate tectonics."

"Daddy! What's that got to do—"

"Hush." He pats the seat. "It's a theory that underneath all this rock and land and rivers that we see, there are plates. That's what everything rests on. Now, these plates have continued to drift for millions of years. Every time a plate bangs up and smashes against another, we get an earthquake. Or sometimes we get something like the Himalayas. That's just a piece of Africa that broke off and smashed into Asia."

"That's crazy!"

"That's what everyone said. When these scientists proposed their theory, everyone said no."

"So what happened?"

"Over time, people began to change how they saw things. Just three years ago, my professor published an article. Even though people had been talking about plate tectonics for decades, the scientific community finally accepted it. They realized it explained so much. Not just the little things going on in one region. But all over. My little island, that's where the Caribbean and Atlantic plates collided.

"Even these cliffs right here. When the earth was made up of just one continent and began to pull apart, hot magma thrust up here and then cooled." He laughs. "This theory is a kind of revolution."

I swing my foot. Interesting, but I have no idea why he's telling me this.

"Sometimes we get so caught up in the little things that are happening to us, maybe we don't understand there's something bigger at play. Bigger forces."

"Like my school?"

"They use a lot of big words. *Integration. Social change. Justice.* We're asking you kids to take on all these big things that we adults can't get right." He sighs. "We're just people. Stones, pebbles. Caught up in something bigger."

"Like tectonics."

"Yes. But not just the actual forces shifting around us." He taps the side of his head. "It's our capacity to see it. To allow ourselves a new way of seeing. That's the real revolution. How we see and think so we can look at something anew."

It takes a while for my father's words to settle. I can imagine him as a boy, hiking the jagged rocks of his island. Daddy reminds me of my art teacher, making us see differently. What they both say makes a kind of sense.

"Weren't you scared?" I ask.

"When?"

"When you met Mom's parents? Grandpa Joe?"

"Darling, there were so many other things I was scared of. Leaving my village. I had never been on an airplane before! And when I landed here, I didn't know if they could understand me! I asked where the lift was and they gave me a look like I was mad.

176

"When it came time to face your mother's family—"
He shrugs. "After supper, your mother wanted to take a
walk. Show me the ice-cream shop and her elementary
school. So we did." He chuckles. "And we held hands, like
we always do. I can't tell you the number of stares. One
man, he slowed down his car and he said, 'You don't do
that! That's against the law!'"

"How can you laugh about it?" I cry.

"What was I supposed to do? Throw a rock? Whatever
I would say would not change that man's mind. What I
could do was live my life with my wife. Believe things
change in the long run."

"In social studies I learned about a court case."

"Glad to hear you're learning something in that
school."

"I heard that it was illegal for you and Mom to marry
in a bunch of states. Until 1967!"

He nods. "That's true."

"But that's like, five years ago!"

"I know."

I pause. "Am I illegal?"

He grins. "No, darling. You are the future."

We go silent. It's peaceful here, a wall of solid carved
rock below us, a rusty barge slowly plying the water. I
can imagine the icebergs carving the slow-moving river
in front of us. Seeing this way—the deeper and longer
structure of the world—I understand why my father stays
so calm.

"I can't be brave like you," I say in a quiet voice.

"You are brave, Jamila. You just don't know it yet."

"I'm not!" And then I sob.

Daddy hugs me tight. I bury my face in his shoulder, keep crying. For all that crossing over, day after day. That bus. The exhausting things me and Josie and Francesca put up with. The weird questions in kindergarten. Eyes gliding over us at the lunch table. The shame I feel around John, knowing that having a white mother has spared me in ways he's not.

We aren't heroes. We're us, in between.

I wipe my face on my sleeve.

"You know," he says, draping his arm around the back of the bench, "it's a lot easier to be on one side or the other. It's harder to be in the middle. People don't like the middle. That's the bravest thing of all."

CHAPTER 24

LETTER

In May everything speeds up at school. I throw myself into electing Johanna. If Josie can mouth off to Darren, I can do the same for Johanna, in a good way. During lunchtime I drop flyers on people's laps. *Vote for Johanna,* they say. *She Gets Things Done!* Lucy rolls her eyes. The twins, Lonnie and Ronnie, ask all kinds of questions, like "Can't we dissect something more than fetal pigs?" and "What about new warming lamps and a greenhouse?"

"She's just a student," I say. "I don't think she can do anything about that."

And I finally do a research project for Mrs. Marko-witz, for real. While my mom shops on Jamaica Avenue on a Saturday, I go to the local history room at the library and pull out old metal flats, poring over city maps and pamphlets. I decide to write about the trolley line that ran all the way from the north to the south of the borough, down to the Rockaways, where people dipped their feet in the coarse sand, or ate ice cream under striped awnings. There were tracks and routes connecting us in some way. Not splitting us up. I even make a funny cartoon about it, with a girl sitting cross-legged on the trolley roof, waving.

When I give Mrs. Markowitz my report, she brightens. "I've got something for you."

She slides open her drawer and hands me my Objective-Subjective notebook. Seeing the cartoons of her and the little angry comments beneath, it feels familiar, but also, from so long ago. I'm annoyed at that girl who wrote this. She was angry and that was all.

The third week in May, after everybody votes, Mrs. Johnson calls me and Johanna into her office. She points to a board where she's tallied the results. Johanna has won—by a lot.

For the first time, I see Johanna lose her cool. She drops her bag, jumps and squeals. She even bends down to kiss my cheek.

"Is that a thank-you?" I ask.

"It sure is!"

After the election, Johanna is even more conceited, sailing down the hall, waving to other kids as if she's in some motorcade. I don't mind as much as before. She kind of deserves it, and who didn't think Johanna would go far in life? Sometimes I think I'll wake up and discover she's running the school.

I wish the long ride would get easier. But every time we're on that bus, something scrapes me inside. Especially if I spot John in the yard. And then one afternoon I am dawdling on the steps with Johanna when he comes right up to me.

"Where you get those?" he asks, pointing to my new sneakers. Josie and Francesca and Jill have written on the white rubber part, their inky letters curling around the edges.

"Jamaica Avenue."

"They're cool."

"Thanks."

We look at each other. The place in my heart is too tender for words.

"See you," he finally says, and walks off, with a bashful wave.

Johanna shifts closer. "Don't worry. He's not going with anyone." She adds, "Not even Tanisha."

I swallow. "Who cares."

Johanna says, "No, really. He's a good guy."

"I guess."

Inside, I think: He's just John, with the sweet smile. Not a boy who is mine.

* * *

In June the principal announces we're having a seventh grade Moving On ceremony, where they'll give out awards. No one understands why seventh graders need a ceremony. We sit in the sweat-slick seats, twisting and fanning ourselves with programs, listening to Mr. Stotter talk about what *a great experiment* we are and to *keep fighting the good fight*. Tanisha wins the best art award, and when she takes it from Mrs. Johnson she stops, blinking as if she's going to cry. Ronnie and Lonnie share the science award, of course; their faces wrinkle into smiles.

It's time for our dance number—Johanna is supposed to lead in the very front, the rest of us in formation in the back. Then I notice Johanna in a corner of the stage wing. She's leaning over and breathing hard. I go over. "What's wrong?"

"I'm scared." She takes a gulp of air. "I didn't know I'd be scared."

I put a hand on her shoulder. She's trembling. "Don't worry," I whisper. "You'll do great."

She gives me a weak smile. "It's just Mr. Sloan. All of them. They put so much pressure on me."

"We're right behind you. Just look over."

The lights dim. We scurry onto the stage and the theme song to *Mission: Impossible* starts to play. Johanna thrusts her arms high, though every now and then she glances at me. I nod. I even sway into the music, do a decent sashay. When the curtains sweep shut, I rush over and put my arms around her. I feel Johanna's sweat and trembling, how small and big she is too.

*   *   *

The next day, I get why we had our ceremony.

I'm working in Mrs. Johnson's office when she hands me a mimeograph. "Make enough for all the kids," she says, her voice tight.

"All?"

"Yes."

I begin to read.

Dear Parents,

I wish to inform you that the district plan to send students to JHS 241 has been discontinued. I know this may be a disappointment for some and that many of you may worry that the disruption will affect the continuity of your child's education. Please know that all efforts are being made to make this as smooth a transition as possible. The junior high that our bused students were originally zoned for is being refurbished this summer to welcome them back.

This year at JHS 241 has been one of

enormous change and educational innovation.
Our staff has done an outstanding job. It
has been my honor to serve your children
and see how they have grown and progressed.
The friendships that were forged and the
life lessons learned within these walls
will stay with our students forever.

Yours,
James Stotter
Principal

I blink, stunned, the purple-blue print swims before me. I'm not even sure why I'm upset. We get to go back to a school in our neighborhood. No more long bus rides, no more hours scooped out of my day. But finally everything is a little bit better. Darren. Johanna. The study club. It's not perfect, but I've found a way to be on both sides somehow. I think: John. I'll never walk down his block with him in the June sun, as if it's no big deal.

I hear Mrs. Johnson behind me. She clears her throat. "I guess I won't be seeing you after this June," she says gently.

I nod, my face hot. "Why did they give up so fast?"

"These plans are hard to pull off. And not everyone was on board." She adds, "I will be keeping an eye on you, though."

"But I'll be at a different school! Far away!"

184

"I have my ways." She sets her hand on my shoulder. I lean toward her a moment, grateful. For the first time, I feel as if an adult here is talking to me, just me, and not as someone to live up to big lofty words and ideas that are so hard to reach.

"Go on," she whispers. "Let's get those letters done."

* * *

At dinner that night my mother explains that she's learned that, because of the complaints, protests, and the petition, a decision was made by the district that the new school "was not benefiting the children."

Karim scowls as he cuts into his meat. But he doesn't say much.

The next day, everyone is buzzing about the news. At lunch Darren uses his lunch tray to point at me and Josie. "No more stuck-up girls. What am I going to do without you bossing me around?"

"I don't know!" I laugh.

He makes a face. "Guess I still got Johanna telling me what to do."

I find Ronnie and Lonnie and Jill sitting in glum silence, picking at their food. Josie looks upset.

"I told you it wouldn't last," Lucy declares. "The busing plan was a bad idea."

Josie and I glance at each other. Then I lean toward the center of the table. "Says who?" I ask.

Lucy reddens. "Just about everybody!"

"And who's everybody?"

"My parents and all the other parents and—" She waves her hand at our table, over the whole lunchroom. "Them too!"

I wince at *them*. But that word, like a lot of words, I have to swallow, and move on. Don't let the little things hurt. But the heat boils up inside, and I get up and stand over Lucy, fists at my sides.

"Jamila—" Josie warns.

"You know what?" I say. "You're wrong. Maybe this didn't work out, but you . . ."

"Yes?" she taunts. She's waiting for me to curse or say something bad.

"You're not the future!"

Lucy's mouth opens and shuts. "I don't even know what that means!"

"I know," I say. "That's the point."

And I walk away.

* * *

The last day, after I've emptied my locker, I come upon Miss Griffith taking down posters outside the gym. "Hey, hon, you okay?"

"It's so unreal."

"I know." She shakes her head, her big hoop earrings swinging against her neck. "Dreams are unreal."

Then she gives me one of her hugs, only this time she takes a little bit longer, so her smoky-sweet scent lingers.

186

We all tumble down the steps into the blazing sunlight, talking and arguing. Nobody wants the time to really end. Then I see John striding toward me. That old butterfly feeling flutters inside.

"So maybe we can visit," he says.

My face lights up. "Yes! We can go to Jamaica Avenue. My mom says—"

"John!"

It's Tanisha. She grins at me. "Y'all back together again?"

We look at each other.

"Don't know," we say at the same time.

Then we laugh. Belly laughs, like when we used to talk on the phone.

The bus driver presses on the horn.

"Up and at 'em, ladies and gentlemen!" Mrs. Johnson yells.

We straggle into the hot bus, groaning under our heavy backpacks, all the extra papers and projects stuffed under our arms.

The bus grinds away. We watch the building grow smaller. I can make out Darren, trying out handsprings for a bunch of other kids. I can hear Jill sniffling behind me. She's lost the twins, her best friends. And me and Josie are returning to our own neighborhood, bad and good. And then I'm crying, more than I ever thought I would, as we turn a corner and the school disappears.

CHAPTER 25

THE LONG RIDE

We agree to wear halter tops, all three of us, though our moms make us put on cardigans. "It's air-conditioned in the bus," Josie's mother says, but that's not the real reason. We know she doesn't want us showing off too much skin.

We pick up Francesca last. It's different in her house: now the parquet floor is stripped of rugs, fewer pretty vases and lamps. And her mother is up early, making breakfast for Francesca. She's different—blond hair pulled back into a ponytail, no makeup. She looks both younger and older.

"You guys want eggs?" she asks. Francesca says her mom started a new job in the city—working at a modeling agency, on the office side. On weekends Francesca crawls into her mom's bed and they sleep in and then make breakfast. Francesca sees her dad in the city on Sundays.

"Sure."

We sit down, dipping our buttery toast in the egg yolks. We all agree that Francesca's mom makes better eggs than at Patty's, though we miss the comic books.

"Francesca, you have enough money for today?" Mrs. George asks.

"Yes, Mom."

"And you'll call once you get there?"

"I said I would!"

"Good." She smiles and kisses the top of Francesca's hair. Francesca leans against her mother, their arms draped around each other. They look almost like sisters.

Then we're out the door, walking through Cedar Gardens. Kids are playing Red Light, Green Light in a courtyard, thumping balls over in the playground. A cluster of boys do wheelies down the road. They seem so young, free.

We stand at the corner, waiting. When the city bus comes roaring up, we drop our tokens in, listen to them twirl down the chute. An old lady with a shopping cart eyes us and smiles. "You going far?"

"Not too far," I say.

"Far," Francesca says at the same time.

"The first time I rode a bus by myself," she explains, "cost a nickel. And it was a streetcar. Not a bus."

I smile, thinking of my research project. I go quiet. This bus ride feels different from the school ride. We're on our own.

When we reach our stop and clamber down the steps, the muggy air hits us.

"My hair!" Francesca wails. She wriggles out of her cardigan and stuffs it into her bag. I do the same. Josie looks cautious. Then she shrugs hers off and gives it to Francesca to put away.

We walk past a row of stores, the little candy shop where the man was so nice. The more we walk, the happier I become, summer starting to feel good on our newly long legs and bare shoulders. We stroll arm in arm, showing our skin, brown and copper and mahogany. We blend and are apart. We won't let anyone make us feel wrong anywhere.

* * *

I recognize the house and tidy yard. And then there's John, coming down the driveway with a hose in his hand, Darren loping behind. "You made it!" John calls out. I'm suddenly warm all over.

John's high-tops are so clean, they're almost blinding.

"New?" I ask.

"Yeah."

"I told him they going to get dirty in two seconds," Darren says.

"Not if you leave me alone," John says.

"That right?" Darren lunges for the hose, rushes to turn on a spigot. Arcs of water spray John, and then us. We shriek and dodge, running into the yard. After a while we flop down on the grass.

"You get your letter?" Darren asks Josie. He means the summer program.

"Yeah."

"You going to do it?" I ask him.

"I'll make him do it," Josie says.

Darren grins. "Good."

We talk some more about the summer, drops of water drying on our arms. Francesca will be off to England in August, but without her mother, who has to work. John is waiting for his brother, Ronald, to come home from the army and then they'll visit family in North Carolina. These days my parents' worries have shifted in another direction: What will happen when Karim gets his draft number in another year? We're going to drive up to Canada to stay with relatives and maybe see about Karim living with second cousins of my father, who immigrated to Toronto. It tears my father up. "It's a nasty business, this war in Vietnam. I didn't raise my son to run away."

"Y'all better keep in touch," Darren says. " 'Specially since Josie and me are sweating it out."

"I'll send you a postcard from Canada," I say. "Snow and mountains. Though it won't be cold then."

"I better get that postcard."

"Sure."

"We won't be together for me and Jamila's birthdays," Francesca says sadly.

"We'll celebrate in the fall," I say.

The screen door flaps open. "Anyone here hungry?"

Nana stands on the back steps in a blue dress, holding up a pitcher of lemonade and shaking a tub of ginger cookies.

I jump up. "Yes!"

Next door I hear voices, someone skipping rope. There's a scent of cut grass. A bus rumbles past a few blocks away. White socks sway on a laundry line. All around us is the smell and feel of summer, of turning thirteen, tipping us forward.

AUTHOR'S NOTE

This novel is a work of fiction. It is based on a busing plan that was implemented in my neighborhood in Queens, New York, in the late sixties and early seventies. I grew up hearing about it from the older kids, and I watched the controversy divide my community. I also drew from my experiences attending diverse public schools. A social studies teacher did take away my journal and read it out loud. And I was picked on for having a beau who was black and told to "stay with my own race." At the time, I was speechless, especially since my race wasn't obvious to me. This book is my attempt to finally speak to some of those experiences.

When we think of integration, we usually think of the iconic images of the National Guard accompanying nine students to school in Little Rock, Arkansas, or of black children being bused into white neighborhoods. Yet the story is much more complex—and it is ongoing.

In 1954, in the *Brown v. Board of Education of Topeka* decision, the U.S. Supreme Court unanimously ruled that a segregated education was not an equal one. But change was slow, and in the 1970s it was clear that our nation's schools remained as segregated as ever. All over the country, school districts experimented with different plans to foster integration. In 1971, the Supreme Court ruled that busing could be used to achieve desegregation. Some plans faltered or provoked bitter protests and riots, as in Boston between 1974 and 1976. Some plans were successful. Former U.S. attorney general Eric Holder, who grew up in Queens, was selected to attend a gifted program in a white school and often speaks of this as a wonderful educational and social experience. Going to that school shaped who he became.

What is often forgotten in the story of desegregation is that children are the ones who must carry out these experiments. While in the 1960s the fight for civil rights was often captured in large events covered in national news, in the 1970s it played out in ordinary neighborhoods, where people struggled, imperfectly, to live out those grand ideals. Schools carried the burden of integration, while the rest of people's lives—where they lived and worked and who they socialized with—remained deeply segregated.

We have yet to meet the challenge of integrating our

schools, along with our cities and towns; today, many districts around the nation, including those in New York City, are more segregated than ever, and the NYC Department of Education is still trying to address inequities. Change doesn't come easily.

Integration is not just a black and white issue; it is also about those of us who do not fit into neat racial categories and who may have been the first to "integrate" schools simply by moving into white neighborhoods. This is sometimes called the "Loving Generation," referring to the U.S. Supreme Court decision *Loving v. Virginia,* which in 1967 struck down the law forbidding interracial marriage in the state of Virginia. That ruling nullified similar laws in fifteen states. For me—of mixed race, with parents who taught in public schools—the conflicts and hopes of this period in large part shaped my coming-of-age. By the time I went to high school, some of these initial clashes around integration had subsided. But even in my own highly integrated high school, there was internal resegregation—an issue that schools struggle with to this day.

The integration plan portrayed in this novel is like many of the clumsy first collisions: well-meaning but unsuccessful. Yet that can't be the end of the story. Studies show that students of color who attend integrated schools tend to do better academically than those who don't. And it's not just minority children who benefit, but all children: a Columbia University Teachers College study found that those who had experienced desegregation "found it to be one of the most meaningful experiences of their lives, the best—and sometimes the only—opportunity to meet and interact regularly with people of different backgrounds."

If you learn to know and love someone of a different race and ethnicity, they won't be a stereotype or an "other" in your mind. You will truly know your own country in all its wonderful diversity. That's the greatest education and gift we can give our children.

ACKNOWLEDGMENTS

Thank you to Darcy Hall for sharing her experience with the I.S. 8 pairing plan, warts and all, and to Jim Hendler for sharing memories and documents from his father Samuel Hendler's archive.

As always, I want to thank my dream team of Wendy Lamb and Dana Carey. Dana, in particular, pushed me hard this time around. To my older son, Sasha, thank you for your perspective and for showing me how we have and haven't moved on from the seventies. My husband, as always, was my sounding board for so much, and reminded me of Albers's color theory. Living with middle schooler Rafi helped me keep the touch light in this book.

Sadly, my mother, Shirley Budhos, did not live to see this novel finished. I've always known this book would be dedicated to her. My mother taught me how to read before I began school, implanting in me not just a love of books but a sense of taking possession of one's own knowledge and learning. She always spoke frankly about race and taught me not to be afraid to speak up about uncomfortable issues.

And we also always went shopping on Jamaica Avenue!

ABOUT THE AUTHOR

Marina Budhos is the author of several award-winning adult and YA novels, including *Watched, Ask Me No Questions,* and *Tell Us We're Home.* With her husband, Marc Aronson, she wrote *Eyes of the World: Robert Capa, Gerda Taro, and the Invention of Modern Photojournalism* and *Sugar Changed the World: A Story of Magic, Spice, Slavery, Freedom, and Science.* She lives in a book-filled house in Maplewood, New Jersey, where she can often be found reading on her front porch.

marinabudhos.com